P9-AOI-966

LADYCAT

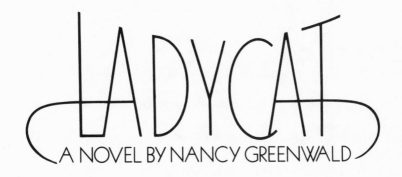

LADYCAT

A NOVEL BY NANCY GREENWALD

CROWN PUBLISHERS, INC.
NEW YORK

Inquiries should be addressed to
Crown Publishers, Inc.,
One Park Avenue,
New York, New York 10016

Printed in the United States of America

Published simultaneously in Canada by General Publishing Company Limited

Library of Congress Cataloging in Publication Data

Greenwald, Nancy.
Ladycat.

I. Title.
PZ4.G8148Lad [PS3557.R3967]   813'.54   79-25665
ISBN: 0-517-541025

10 9 8 7 6 5 4 3 2 1

FIRST EDITION

Book Design: Shari de Miskey

For Robert

LADYCAT

ANTONIA
1.

IF IT IS AT ALL POSSIBLE TO RACE OUT OF THE house with a three-year-old hellion, a stroller that refuses to collapse, lunch for two in separate brown bags, a stack of Russian history books, and touchy-feely books for a child, then I raced. A more accurate description would be to say that we stumbled down three flights of stairs before reaching the outer stoop. Rachel fell and cried only once. By the time we got to the bus stop I was a wreck and she was ecstatic because she had unnerved me.

I had left behind two unmade beds and a stack of dirty dishes in the kitchen sink. I like having a neat house; when I come home from school I feel reassured when I turn on my kitchen light and see nothing but shiny counter tops. I believe in spic-and-span, although I am ashamed to admit it. My husband had been very sloppy. He left a trail of crumbs behind him wherever he went. I followed in his tracks with a wet sponge. We parted company anyway, and Michael left Berkeley to hitch cross-country. He wound up in the Midwest somewhere, working a small farm with a dull blond couple. All three have become involved in religion and are continually going off on retreats.

There is no child support. Rachel and I struggle through as best we can. She goes to Wendy's Place, a day-care center on Sacramento Street, four to six hours a day, and I go to UC Berkeley as a graduate fellow in Russian history (with strong preference for dance). Which is to say I have practically no money at all. Graduate fellows receive a small stipend that they're supposed to live on for the year, but most people can't make it on that pittance. I not only support myself but a child as well, which is why Rachel and I were waiting at that bus stop. I would have loved to drive her to day care, but my car had broken down the preceding week and I couldn't afford to have it fixed. It was sitting in the junkyard because no one had wanted it in its sorry state.

The bus driver was furious at me for trying to get a stroller that doesn't fold up into the bus, and it didn't help any when I tried to explain that the folding mechanism was broken. I told him I minded more than he did, and he told me not to be a wise ass. Rachel kept running to the front of the bus and calling him "daddy" and asking him, "Daddy, please c'n I sit on your lap?" or "Daddy, lemme drive, please?" I was relieved when we got to our stop.

I dropped her off on the corner because I owed Wendy for three months of child care and I wasn't in the mood to hassle with her about it. It wasn't until I was sitting in class that I remembered I had left my house keys on the kitchen table. Jesus! How was I ever going to get back into the building? My next-door neighbor was no longer speaking to me because she was convinced I kept forgetting my keys on purpose, and the super didn't live in the building. Besides, the keys I had left at home on the kitchen table were his—I borrowed them the preceding week and had forgotten to have another set made up.

"Ms. Weiner. Could you come out of your reverie long enough to tell me the Russian peasants' response to the statutes of February 19, 1861, according to Florinsky?"

"I'm sorry. I forgot my keys again and I don't know how I'll get back into my apartment."

My three male classmates were terribly amused by my response and guffawed and cackled like a bunch of baboons. I felt like an ass. Nevertheless, I went on to answer Professor Warren's question brilliantly. Only it didn't mean anything to any of them because all they could think about was this dingbat of a woman who kept coming out with non sequiturs in class.

Dance class was a special relief that afternoon. Every fiber in my body was concentrated on getting the muscles moving with the beat, flowing with the rhythms of each new exercise. The muscles fell in line moving up my back, from my waist to the top of my neck as I released the first time, and Jeffrey, my friend/mentor/teacher, had to tell me to get that dopey grin off my puss. I'm always convinced that I walk into the dance room a jangle of nervous energy, the muscles across my shoulders knotted up from the various tensions of my life, but that it all melts away with the first contraction/release. I can't help but smile some days. We did some very intricate steps going across the floor and I was in top form. Jeffrey even asked me to demonstrate each new turn, bend, twist, and leap with him. As I was leaving the room at the end of class, he paid me a glorious compliment.

"My dear, your body melted into mine as we glided across that room, today. Are you sure you can't be persuaded to join my company, Antonia?"

I laughed but told him no. My true calling was as a Ph.D., not as a fledgling dancer in a San Francisco dance company.

I showered and changed and crossed campus on the run because I was behind schedule. As soon as I opened the door to Wendy's Place, I knew something was up: Rachel was stretched out on a mat across the room, holding her favorite doll in her arms. My child is a mover; she never lies down until I force her to because I'm ready to collapse. Wendy intercepted me as I ran across the room.

"She started to feel sick in the park, Tony; she's pretty warm. I already called Doctor Ragan for you, and he said you could bring her by on your way home."

4

I knelt down to feel her forehead and, indeed, she was pretty warm. She put her arms around me and started to whimper. My poor baby.

Wendy stroked the back of her head while I kissed her on the forehead.

"You want me to get you a cab?" Wendy was very thoughtful.

I shook my head yes and continued rocking my child. By the time we arrived at the doctor's office, she was hot. When the doctor tickled her tummy and kissed her neck, she didn't even laugh. He examined her as quickly as possible and discovered she was not only congested but had an infected ear as well; she needed penicillin. Her last ear infection had lasted a week and a half: she had been in a lot of pain. I wanted to get her to bed and rush right over to the drugstore, pick up the miracle drug, and start it rolling down her precious little throat.

It wasn't till the cab dropped us on College Avenue, a half block from our apartment building, that I remembered I didn't have my keys. I set Rachel down on the stoop, wrapped my coat around her shoulders, and told her to sit tight: somehow I'd get the door open and come on down for her.

Ringing the doorbell of the kid down the hall turned out to be a good idea. He buzzed back and the front door opened. I jammed a book in between the door frame and door, ran back out for Rachel, and set her down against the foyer wall. I raced up the stairs two at a time but didn't have a notion of how I would get into our apartment by the time I reached our floor.

Rach and I live on the top floor of an old Berkeley

apartment building, three apartments to a floor. There are no fire escapes, which is a shame, since I would have used them with great frequency. I sat against my door to think; it was pretty drafty. Then I got a brainstorm.

The heat in our apartment can't be regulated, so I open the kitchen window every morning when I get up. Of course, in my haste to get to class that morning, I had forgotten to close the window, I yelled down to Rachel to stay put—I would only be a few minutes more—then hiked on up to the roof. I walked over to the ledge at the spot I presumed my kitchen to be under and peered over.

I almost passed out. My stomach moved up to my throat and I had to sit down and lean back against the ledge itself. I forced myself to look again. If I sort of leaned out over the ledge and down, with my head up-side down, I could almost look into the top of my kitchen window. There was my pail of Spic and Span sitting next to the stove, right where I had left it, and the dirty, egged-up dishes in the sink. I stood up and groaned.

Was I really in good enough shape to do it? I didn't know, but the drugstore closed at seven and it was already a quarter to six. I told myself to get moving, adding, "This is really nuts," to the world in general, and bequeathed my books, records, and kid to Wendy, should my plan fail. Then I climbed on top of the ledge, faced in, knelt down, grasped the ledge with my hands, and slowly let myself down, shimmying into place until I was suspended by my hands, feet dangling.

Unfortunately, they didn't quite reach my window

ledge. I looked down. I was only short by a couple of inches. I had to make a quick decision, because my arms hurt and the fingers on my left hand felt a bit numb. Since I didn't think I could chin myself back up to the roof, the only alternative seemed to be to let go and try to land on the window sill. If I lost my balance, I would just dive through the bottom half of my open window.

I let go—and found myself staring into our lovely, red and off-white kitchen. I grabbed the upper frame of the window, bent my knees, lowered my tush onto the window ledge, and sat down. Then I leaped into the middle of the room, landing in fifth position, smiling, very proud of myself and relieved as hell to be inside in one piece. As I ran down the three flights for Rachel, I found myself humming Purcell's *Music for Trumpet and Orchestra*. Rach hugged me all the way back up and then helped me pull down her covers and tumble her under them. We got her pajamas on without any major mishaps, I brought her a bottle (which she only uses when she's sick—I guess it makes her feel less horrible, somehow), put on "Tubby the Tuba," and sat on the edge of her bed waiting for her to doze off. It took exactly six minutes. I called the druggist by 6:05.

The old man who owned the store had already gone home: his assistant was an unpleasant kid just out of pharmacy school. He informed me I already owed his boss $12.50. The new medicine would bring the bill to $21.00. Unless I brought in the full amount, he couldn't give me the medicine. I begged the bastard not to penalize my kid because of the hour of the day (how could I get to my bank?), but he was unmoved.

"Borrow the bread from a neighbor, lady," came the gruff reply, and then he hung up. It was already 6:20.

I was pretty damned upset. Quickly I ran next door, but my neighbor had only a few dollars in change on her. I rang doorbells, but no one else on the floor seemed to be home. My throat was developing a huge lump. I sat down on the living room couch. Rachie groaned in her sleep; I got up and poured myself a glass of wine from the Almadén carafe Wendy had left me on the window sill after her last visit. She knows I am too poor to buy it for myself and that I dearly love wine.

My glance swept across the alley, and before I could do anything about it, I realized I was looking into some stranger's apartment. It was pretty dark, and the window was open. I looked up at the roof. It had the same kind of ledge my roof did.

Without thinking about it at all, I slipped on my ballet shoes and ran around the corner. I had to hurry to beat the seven o'clock deadline and get back home before Rachie woke up. She was sleeping pretty fitfully, and her little face was awfully flushed. I think maybe I momentarily flipped out or something, because suddenly I found myself hanging over this roof, peering into a strange dining room. I pliéd to the window sill, did a quick little tumble into the room, and rolled right into an old and very rickety dining room chair. I lay there very sick to my stomach, but nothing happened. If anyone was home, he or she was obviously asleep.

I got up quietly and looked around. There didn't seem to be anything much of value in the dining room—just some old chairs, a junky bridge table, and the standard prints on the wall. The kitchen had little more to offer. The silverware was from Newberry's, as were the plates. Someone had left $2.57 on the kitchen counter top, and I pocketed it. It wasn't enough.

I turned toward the hall, stopped, and held my breath. I thought I heard a noise. It must have been only several seconds that I stood there, but it felt like hours. No one came into the kitchen and nothing moved, so I tiptoed down the hall as fast as I could. I opened the first door I came to—it creaked slightly, but the sound reverberated in my ears—and found myself in some guy's bedroom. I knew it was a guy because I heard him snoring.

My instinct was to turn and run because he might wake up, and what the hell would I do then, but I forced myself to stand still. I turned my head and scanned the room. Over on the dresser I was sure I could make out the shape of his wallet. I inched over to the blob in the dark with my chest aching. I hadn't taken a breath in moments; I was afraid the noise of my breathing would wake the snorer.

For once in my life, I lucked out. The guy had over fifty bucks in his wallet—he must have gone to the bank that day. It was tempting as hell to take the whole thing, but I reminded myself that I had only come for the money to pay for Rachie's drugs. I took out nineteen dollars—counting the change would have been too noisy—put the wallet back where I had found it, and made a hasty but quiet exit. I left by the front door and ran around the corner and up the stairs back to my place.

I called the pharmacy student, told him I had borrowed the money, and asked him to deliver. He told me the store was about to close. He begged me to stop crying and assured me he would drop the medicine off on his way home. I hung up and poured myself some more wine. I had to sit down, because my legs were shaking so badly I didn't think they'd be able to support my weight much longer. I was too exhausted to feel any tension anyplace else.

By the time the guy arrived I was having my third glass of wine and couldn't hold the spoon still enough to pour. He fed Rachel her medicine while I stroked her forehead, but declined the glass of wine I offered him, assuring me my child would be fine in the morning.

"You don't have to be so nervous. It's just another ear infection."

I smiled at him with genuine relief, thinking to myself never again! I ushered him out and followed his advice, practically falling into bed.

Much to my surprise, I slept very well that night, although by the time I woke up my stomach seemed to be orchestrating a new *Mass* by Bernstein. On my way to Rach's room, I stopped at the medicine chest for some Maalox and popped two tabs in my mouth. Actually, I am probably one of the few people on this earth who likes Maalox, mainly because it always makes me feel better. Rachel's breathing was pretty smooth and she didn't look very flushed anymore.

I put up a pot of Sanka, sliced two bagels in half, cut up a grapefruit, and scrambled some eggs. Then I sat down to think about what I had done the night before and why.

First I tried to quell my rising hysteria by assuring myself that what had happened was a once-in-a-lifetime aberration. It had been worth it because Rachel was no longer wheezing in her sleep, but it would never happen again.

Nevertheless, I couldn't keep the thought out of my head that if she had gotten sick at two in the afternoon, we wouldn't have been any better off. I still wouldn't have been able to pay for those drugs. The only money I had in reserve was the five dollars I had used on the cab fare to and from the doctor's office. My account at Wells Fargo was empty; had I written a check, it would have bounced.

The first few months after Michael left, Rach and I had survived on my fellowship. Things had been tight, but I always managed to have a little extra; a couple of dollars here, a few more there, for ice cream or berries or some other Rachel-treat. The past few months, however, had been something else.

I tried to eat some of the scrambled eggs and almost choked. "Of course, your financial situation has gotten worse, dummy!" I swore at myself. Those first few months a neighbor with a little girl a couple of months younger than Rach had taken my child in for nothing the few hours a day I was at Cal. Then she enrolled in graduate school, too, and started sending her kid to Wendy's Place. I had no choice but to follow suit. By then Rach and Nicole were inseparable. Before I could turn around, I found myself shelling out twenty dollars a week for day care. There went my tiny cash reserve.

The first few months Rach was at Wendy's Place, I paid for it out of my savings. Then I borrowed some money from Jeffrey, which put a severe strain on our friendship. When that ran out, I stopped paying Wendy altogether. She was being very nice about it because she knew how hard I was struggling to keep on top of it all. I had never sat down to examine my plight because I had always managed to muddle through before. That was beginning to seem like a bad way to operate. Not being able to afford twenty-one dollars for medicine for my kid was absurd.

Right after Michael had left Berkeley, I had put up signs offering dance classes at two dollars an hour to little girls eight to ten years old. There had only been two responses, and Rach and I seemed to be surviving okay, what with Nicole's mom and the little I had borrowed, so I had canned the whole idea. Now seemed like a good time to resurrect it.

I tiptoed in to look at Rachel again. She opened her eyes and immediately grinned a huge grin, stumbling to her feet so she could give me her morning hug. Her forehead was cool, so I figured it was okay to drop her at Wendy's. That, plus my decision to start teaching dance, lifted my sagging spirits.

When we got to the church that houses Wendy's Place, I explained to Wendy that Rachie seemed much better and needed to take her penicillin every four hours. I handed her the brown bottle and raced off before she could bring up the question of the money I owed her. Owing money was one thing I didn't need to hear about that particular day. The "incident" of the night before was a thing of the past.

Two girls with very short hair and a sign on their

bumper, saying Give a Ride to a Sister, picked me up at Sacramento and Cedar, so I got to campus a little early. Instead of sitting in an empty classroom, which I loathe doing, I stopped by my office to print up my signs announcing the dance lessons. I should explain. "My" office consisted of about five little cubicles, with five ugly uniform desks and not even one file cabinet. There was a hot plate in the next room, and one guy in my office kept bouillon cubes around, another tea and coffee. I borrowed liberally from both of them.

A heavy discussion was going on when I thumped my books down on my desk. My cellmates were all very nice-and-kindly pedantic types. I'll go down the list for you. Dick Farber was over six feet, terribly skinny, with a crew cut and dark brown glasses. He was very earnest. Teddy, the guy who sat next to him, had pretences of being the next Daniel Boorstin, in German history. He played at being radical and had a baby daughter, which prevented him from giving money to, much less participating in, any real radical group. Tom and Leslie were a husband-and-wife team. He was an economic historian (I never have figured out what that meant), and short. She was a head taller and was in "intellectual" history. I was undecided.

I had thought I wanted to teach Russian history, but my advisor, Professor Warren, was a stodgy scholarly type who had real difficulty with the creative bent of my papers—the same quality that made me such a star at Antioch. He was a nice man, so we hadn't had a direct confrontation as yet. He just referred to my "problem" adjusting to graduate school, and I kept my peace. What with my home situation the year before, when I started my studies at Berkeley, and my current financial crisis, I didn't want any extra hassles, although I still wasn't knuckling under all that well. There was a terrific professor—Gelb—in German history, who encouraged creativity, but that would mean changing majors and starting over, and I certainly couldn't do that.

Anyway, Tom and Leslie were complaining to Dick about the injustice of working for minimal wages with absolutely no provision for a disastrous economy and spiraling inflation.

"No one knows slave labor is still going strong in this country. I analyzed the whole thing on my computer. We work for forty-seven cents an hour. Thirty-two cents if you count all the hours we put in at home."

Leslie's whine joined the discussion. "We don't even do anything interesting. All we do is the shit work like grading exams and papers."

"Of course," quipped Tom. "Who would trust us to plan a course? We don't know enough yet."

"And we won't until we're forty and boring assistant professors," groaned Dick.

"It's a rotten system." Teddy got on his pedestal. "We should get a least a thousand bucks a year more for the amount of work we do."

Gloom descended on the room, as it had a hundred times before. Dick offered everyone a bouillon cube; I was the only one to decline. Granted, everything they said was true. They just never came up with any solutions, and that was what I was looking for. I had to post my signs immediately.

After I put signs up in Bancroft, the Union, and

Dwinelle, I went back to my office and spent the rest of the afternoon frantically phoning everyone I knew, to try to dredge up a few committed students to assure myself some kind of weekly income. Jeffrey offered to make an announcement about my class before each of his, and the school paper agreed to run an ad for me for nothing. Several bookstores on Telegraph Avenue posted my signs, and a lady in the dance office thought she knew a lady who had a friend who had kids who might want to take dance classes. Much to my surprise, seven girls had signed up by Friday. Because of the problems of juggling around their schedules of piano lessons, singing lessons, painting lessons, swimming lessons, my class couldn't begin for a week and a half. Still, that would give me time to plan the first couple of classes. I was feeling pretty good when I walked out of my history seminar, and I decided to pick up Rachie instead of doing my usual hour and a half in the library. I ran into Jeffrey as I turned up Durant.

"Tony, my dear. What are you doing out on the street? You're usually in the library reading away at this hour." Jeffrey bounced up to me. His long, thin arm went around my shoulders and he pulled me up the block into the Mediterraneum.

"This time you can't say no. I've got you where I want you. Do you take sugar and cream?"

I couldn't help protesting, "But, Jeffrey, I was planning to work at home . . ." Then I saw the look on his face and gave in.

"Cream, no sugar. Actually, skim milk, if they have it."

He guided me upstairs; we spent forty-five minutes

discussing my plight. As I said before, that one time Jeffrey had lent me money after Michael left had proved disastrous. He felt uncomfortable asking me to pay him back, and I was miserable that I couldn't. After I finally dredged up the money for him, we made an agreement never to go through such a trial again.

So, we concentrated on my dance classes. Jeffrey offered me his room during lunch hour (a good time for me, too) and assured me he could scrounge up at least three more students for me—kids of friends of friends of long lost friends and like that. We toasted my soon-to-be-in-hand wealth with the last of our coffee and walked to the bus stop arm in arm. Jeffrey was beginning to get maudlin about my abilities as a dancer—he usually does after more than one caffè latte. "My dear, I think you could stretch those long legs of yours an extra eight inches and then plié in first without even a grimace."

I burst out laughing—Jeffrey continually complains about the faces I make when I'm working extra hard. As we parted at the curb, he asked me to reconsider joining his company.

"We're receiving small fees wherever we perform nowadays," he assured me sotto voce, so everyone could hear.

Before I could remind him that if I did, I'd never see my kid, the No. 51 came lumbering up to the corner. Jeffrey pushed me up and in, cautioning me, "Don't forget. I'll be by on Sunday to take Little Miss Muffet to the park." I thanked him with a wave.

I think it was my extreme involvement in solving our overall money problems that made me forget Rachel's birthday. It was in six days and I was broke. My dance classes were beginning the following week; maybe she'd be willing to postpone the party for that week, until I had collected my first week's payment. We could have a belated bash and make it extra special. All her school friends could be invited. The idea seemed good to me, so I decided to try it out on her at supper.

"Rachie . . ."

"What, Mommy?"

"Well, honey, I can't afford to give you that little birthday party we talked about for Friday. But if we wait a week, I'll have money from the dance classes I'll be giving, and you'll be able to invite Nicole and Eric and the whole gang. What do you think?"

Rachie sat there for a minute staring at me, and then her eyes squinched up into tiny little slits, her mouth opened wide, and she began to sob. She jerked her chair away from the table, overturning it in her haste to get to her bed. In a few seconds she called out, "My birthday's this Friday, not next week!" and burst into tears again.

I held her on my lap and soothed her and kissed her and told her I was sorry, all the time feeling like a terrible traitor. But what could I do? The way things had turned out, there just wasn't any money to spend that week. All weekend I tried to make it up to her.

Then, on my way to campus Monday, I passed by a gift shop. I stopped a few feet beyond it and retraced my steps. Suddenly I realized I was furious.

"Goddamn it," I thought to myself. "It isn't fair that I can't give Rachie a piddling little birthday party!" I all but marched into the shop.

It didn't take me long to pick out matching paper

plates, cups, and spoons, a cute pin-the-tail-on-the-donkey game, plus some other knickknacks and games for Friday. The bill came to $15.78. I was stunned: for paper goods? That was what the 1½ percent cost increase I had read about in the *Chronicle* was all about. I held my stomach with one hand while I wrote the check. I figured it would take several days to bounce, and by then I'd find a way to get the money to pay for it.

I moved through my dance class like a robot and told Jeffrey I didn't have time for coffee. If I hurried, I'd have just enough time to pick up franks, beans, potatoes for salad, and ice cream at the Co-op. I could charge it there for a few days anyway, because I knew the manager. The bill came to $18.50. I felt a momentary panic—how the hell would I ever get the money to pay for it?—but I pictured Rachie's little red face Friday night and that was that.

I ran all the way to Wendy's Place and scooped the kid up in my arms, dumping the groceries on the floor. I kissed her all over, bent down and took out the little invitations, and kissed her again.

"If we fill them out tonight, you can give them to your friends in the morning. That'll give everyone plenty of notice for Friday."

Rachel stared. "You mean we're having the party?"

I shook my head yes.

"Oh, Mommy; oh, Mommy; oh, Mommy!"

We had a great time with the invitations and I read her three stories before putting her to bed. She even got me to read "Good night, Moon" twice.

After Rachel was in bed, I poured myself some Almadén and sat down in my favorite chair by the fireplace, even though it had no fire.

Okay. Here was the situation. The party had put me into debt, $34.28 worth. I couldn't call Jeffrey after the last time. Anyway, he was more than generous with his time, taking Rachel camping for a whole weekend, playing with her for hours when I was busy, and that was good enough for me. I put all thoughts of monetary aid from him out of my head. Tom and Leslie were paying back the loan they had taken to get her through Berkeley as an undergrad, so they never had an extra penny. I already owed Wendy money, so she was out. Michael was on retreat in the woods and had been unreachable for a couple of months. The only ones left were my parents. I sighed and picked up the phone.

"Hi, Ma."

"Tony! What a pleasant surprise. How's my baby?"

"Well, actually, that's why I'm calling."

"What? Something's the matter?"

"Not really; I mean she's okay physically. She had an ear infection, but the penicillin's working okay."

"Are you sure? You could call Dr. Weissberg, if you want."

"Mother, he's all the way in Short Hills. What could he say from that distance?"

There was a silence at the other end. Finally, she spoke. "So, what's the matter?"

"Rachie's birthday's Friday . . ."

"I know," she interrupted. "Did you get our present?"

"No, not yet. Ma, I promised her a birthday party and I don't have enough cash to pay for it," I burst out before she could break in on me.

"What about that louse, Michael? Doesn't he give you any help?"

I bit my lip and closed my eyes to keep the anger in check. "Ma, you know he doesn't."

"I know. He just runs around in the woods."

"He's not running around, he's . . . goddamn it, he's trying to find God."

"When you got married, he wouldn't even agree to a rabbi."

"Mother, knock it off. People change; that's his right."

I could hear her breathing at the other end. "So how much is it going to cost?"

"About thirty-five dollars."

"That's a lot of money, Antonia."

"I know, Mother."

"Since your father retired, we've been trying to save a little, in case either of us gets sick . . ."

Neither of us said anything until I gave up.

"Okay, Mom, I'm sorry. It's all right, Rachie can get along without a party. Have a nice week. Tell Daddy I said hello."

"I'm sorry, too, Tony. Give her a kiss for us and let us know how she likes the present. Call collect."

We hung up.

My stomach growled but I couldn't keep the thought out of my head anymore. I had lost my Co-op membership once already, and they told me when I renewed it that was the last time. The check would bounce by Wednesday or Thursday and I didn't have the faintest idea what a bank would do if a person couldn't make a bum check good. The party was on Friday and I wanted to be there for it. If I pulled one more little theft, I could pay back the Co-op on time and clear myself with the bank. I felt very trapped and guilty thinking that way, but I really didn't know what else to do.

"So all right. Just one more little job doesn't make me into a dishonest person, a liar, and a cheat," I reasoned to myself. "I have no choice."

By my second glass of wine I had decided that if I was going to burglarize someone again, I would do it as quickly as possible but with a little more care than the first time. I would spend all day Tuesday looking for the right apartment and then case it out carefully on Wednesday. I'd get in and out Wednesday afternoon in time to pay the Co-op and wouldn't take everything the person had, because I could never rob anyone blind. I managed to talk myself into believing the whole thing was a matter of necessity, and I still sort of believe it was.

The next day, I chose a three-story modern building on Hillegas, because I figured with all those occupants, one was bound to be out a lot. First, I picked out open windows, and then I waited around to see who lived behind them. If a lady appeared at a window or turned on a light or pulled down a shade, I crossed it off my list of possibles. I suppose I figured if I ever got caught in the act, as it were, I'd be able to wriggle out of it better with a man.

Anyway, I noticed that there was this guy with jet black hair and a good build, who lived on the second floor of an old ramshackle building across the street. He kept his windows open and went out for hours at a time; he seemed like a good target.

Casing out his apartment wasn't a bad experience. Actually, it fulfilled all the sixth-grade fantasies I had when I used to go over to Judy Tunney's house so that we could walk the short block and a half to Judson Carter's and innocently stroll by. And by and by and by. Once, he came outside and we ran like hell. The adult me walked by "Mr. Jet's" house all day Tuesday, to get a line on his hours and to figure out the best time to strike. I almost gave up the idea of robbing him, preferring instead the fantasy of stealing over his sill and seducing him. Business, however, was business.

"Mr. Jet" had left his apartment for the first time at ten the following morning with a load of books under his arm and had been home by two, carrying more books. He had gone out again at four and come back with groceries at seven thirty. I was debating whether to wait around on the off chance he'd go out again, when he came racing out the front door, throwing on his jacket as he ran down the block. How could I blow such a golden opportunity by waiting until the next day? Wendy took Rachel home with her on Tuesday nights to have dinner with her commune, so it was a perfect setup for me in every way. I watched him round the corner and then followed a few feet behind because I wanted to put in a quick call to Wendy to make sure she could keep Rachie till nine thirty or so. By the time I reached College Avenue he was gone. The phone call took about five minutes because Rachie wanted to tell me what she had eaten for dinner. Wendy's boyfriend had cooked the vegetables in a wok, she informed me. They were poured over brown rice.

"That's better for you than Uncle Ben's, Mommy, and it's cheaper"—she paused briefly—"we're playing . . . um . . . making faces and it's my turn, so I gotta go."

I was back on Hillegas by eight.

He had left the front door of the building open, so it was easy to get up to the roof. I walked to the edge and peered over. He had closed one of his windows, and the only one open had a very narrow ledge. In addition, when I leaned out and over, it became clear to me that the distance from roof to narrow sill was much too long for a woman of normal stature, even a dancer with marvelous extension. I sat down on the ledge of the roof to give it some thought. Damn it, I had really begun to count on getting at least thirty-five dollars that night, so I could pay the Co-op the next day and be done with it. My career as a burglar would be over and I could stop worrying about it. A bird twittered at me from the tree in the backyard and it sounded lovely. My God, the tree.

I stood up to get a better look, and, sure enough, one of the branches came within inches of his open window. Luckily, the tree was in the farthest corner of the yard and wasn't visible from the front. The bottom branch was pretty high up, so I had to lunge at it several times before I could grab onto it firmly; and when I finally connected, it was only with my left, and weaker, hand. I swung back and forth with my legs scraping against the bark until I could grab on with the other hand. It was a good thing I had on my oldest pair of jeans. I pulled myself up by the arms and hooked my legs around the thick, gnarled branch. From there it was easy to get up the tree. The only other tricky moment came when I was edging my way out on the branch. It started to creak and I couldn't decide whether to speed up or get off altogether. I brazened it out and landed in his bedroom by 8:22. As soon as my eyes accustomed themselves to the dark, I started to case out the room.

There was nothing on the bureau top but a dirty, crumpled-up handkerchief. I made my way to the hulking mass outlined against the wall perpendicular to the bureau. It turned out to be an old-fashioned rolltop desk. I tried to pry it open, but the accordian-type rollaway cover needed oiling: it squeaked each time I tried to move it. The noise sounded horrible to me, but apparently no one else heard it because no one came to investigate. Inside, in the top right-hand drawer, was a rawhide wallet. I had a momentary anxiety attack (My God! What if he was home?), but then I realized all the lights were out and I had seen him leave moments before. He couldn't possibly be there. Maybe he had two wallets, I thought to myself. He kept the new one on him and his old one in his desk. To stop myself from agonizing about it, I got down to business and went through the wallet. Christopher. His name was Christopher. What a lovely name. He had Master Charge, BankAmericard, and American Express, plus thirty dollars. I left the cards and pocketed the money.

Probably I should have left right then and there, but I wanted to see if he had any more money lying around. Twenty-five dollars really wasn't enough, and I didn't want to have to rob anyone else. I opened the door to

24

the next room and stepped inside. It was so dark I couldn't see a damn thing. Reaching down, I put my hand on a wet, warm, clammy finger.

"Jesus!" I exclaimed. "What's that?"

A very deep voice quietly replied, "My hand."

"What are you doing here in the dark?"

"Taking my bath. What are you doing in my apartment? You have a nice voice."

"Well, I guess I'm in the wrong apartment. I meant to go next door."

"Who're you visiting?"

"Your next-door neighbor." *Pause.* "You must take a very hot bath; my hair is beginning to crinkle up."

"Put your hand in."

"How can you sit in there? It's burning up."

"A hot bath is really quite invigorating. I do it every night. Helps start my creative juices flowing. Why don't you get in and try it?"

It seemed patently ridiculous to say, "I don't even know you," and he was so attractive I could just picture what he looked like in that large, old-fashioned tub. To tell the truth, my eyes were beginning to accustom themselves to the dark.

I unbuttoned the fly of my jeans, but before I even touched the zipper I was overwhelmed by second thoughts. Taking baths with strangers was going too far. I redid the button.

"What's up?" Mr. Jet sounded curious, and mildly disappointed, when I disregarded his invitation.

"I'm sorry, but I can't. This is not my style. I just can't."

He took my hand in his and placed a bar of soap in it.

25

It was the lovely smelling glycerine kind, but I dropped it back in the tub anyway, sat down on the toilet seat, for lack of anything better to do, and again repeated, "I'm sorry."

"Think nothing of it." Christopher smiled up at me.

I think he was enjoying the whole scene immensely.

"So, what're you doing in my apartment?"

"Do I have to tell you the truth?"

"It would be nice."

"It isn't at all simple. I think I'd have to go into all the background details."

"That's okay with me. I like taking a long bath; I usually do."

"In the dark?"

"Um h'mm. It's more relaxing."

He seemed to be waiting, so I told him the whole thing from beginning to end. I guess I was really anxious to tell someone about this crazy and frightening thing I had gotten involved in, anyhow. Somewhere in the middle, Christopher suggested I turn around, wrapped himself in an orange terry-cloth bathrobe (very snugly), and sauntered down the hall into his kitchen. I followed. He sat down while I opened up the refrigerator. When I saw the fresh vegetables and lamb chops (four of them—a man after my own heart), it seemed proper to prepare dinner, which I did. He didn't object, and having something to do with my hands actually helped me to tell him the story, because it made me less anxious about what he would think. I was too busy making him a good, healthy supper to care.

He ate very well, offering me coffee ice cream for

dessert. I had found a soul mate. I ate almost as well as he did.

"Antonia, you are incredible."

I shrugged. "Just a divorcee from Short Hills."

"Really? I'm from Westfield."

"What a coincidence."

Then neither of us had anything else to say. The room felt very intimate, and I was profoundly uncomfortable. I had never slept with anyone just like that, even in a normal situation, but that's suddenly what I wanted to do. He must have been a mind reader.

"Neither have I, Antonia, so relax."

It was only a few yards to the bedroom and we made it without any mishaps. Luckily, I had never bothered taking out my IUD. After all, there was always a chance. . . .

God, it was beautiful. Not like a first time at all, really. I knew that I enjoyed making love with someone I knew very well, but suddenly I was discovering it was okay with someone I didn't know all that well, too. You know, Christopher really is a very nice person and that must have had something to do with how good it was.

"Antonia, you shouldn't be ripping off your fellow students in Berkeley. I don't know that I think it's intrinsically wrong to steal, but I sure as hell don't think it's your style to do it to your peers."

"I know. This was going to be the last time." I sighed a big sigh.

"What're you going to do for money?"

"I don't know."

"Well, don't worry about the Co-op or the bank. I'll give you the money for that."

I turned beet red and told him I already had his thirty dollars. He laughed a good rich laugh and handed me an additional five dollars from a cup on his counter top. He paused briefly. "Can I see you again?"

"Yes, except I don't want to tell you my last name or give you my address because I'm a little paranoid about tonight. Okay?" I was still horribly uneasy.

"Do you really promise to come over again?"

I shook my head yes.

"Well, then I guess you don't have to give me your number."

I was very happy and couldn't keep from blurting out, "I really like you an awful lot, Christopher."

"Would you meet me for lunch tomorrow?"

"Sure. In the Terrace at twelve thirty?"

"Okay."

"Christopher?"

"What, Antonia?"

God, he smiled a lot. "Are you a student at Berkeley?"

"A lecturer in political science."

McQUADE
2.

IT WASN'T THAT MY CLIENT WAS WORSE
than usual. He was a prick, but his case was well suited to
the talents of Barton, Wells and McDonough, one of San
Francisco's most reputable law firms. Since I was the
firm's firebrand and youngest partner, I had been
selected to defend the case. Maybe old man Barton
thought I was the only one unscrupulous enough to get
him off. Actually, the client, Tom Percy, was a rich son
of a bitch. Par for the course. He ran one of those outfits
in the Mission District that specializes in writing theses
for poor college schnooks who don't think they can do it

themselves. They have been "just getting by" but desperately want to make it through to doctor.

The girl who had brought charges against Percy was a pathetic case. She was plump with an advanced state of teenage acne that had apparently never gone away. In her late twenties, she had a light brown mustache running across her upper lip. The thesis he had written for her hadn't been considered good enough by the anthropology department at Berkeley, and she had been denied her Ph.D.

Ordinarily, I would have had absolutely no sympathy for her. First of all, she was a horror show. Second, she never should have hired anyone to write her thesis for her in the first place. If she went to someone like Percy, she deserved what she got. Percy was immoral, but his clients were stupid, a far worse crime in my book.

But this one was really a sad case. Constantly dabbing at her red-tipped nose with a Kleenex throughout the proceedings, the girl managed to get to me. I'd look at her and then look away.

"Christ," I turned to Percy. "You should have made sure the thesis was A-1 perfect just so you'd never have to see her again."

The son of a bitch merely shrugged. "They're all like that."

"So why do it?"

He couldn't believe his ears. "Why do anything, Mac? To make money, asshole."

So, I had no special love for Percy; he was repulsive. I sat there wondering how many Berkeley Philosophers with a capital *P* owed their degree to him. Judging by his

income, quite a few. Then I thought about myself—
"Mac" to friends or anyone else I happened to find use-
ful. Percy probably wasn't so wrong. What reason could
I have for defending the scumbag other than money.
Fame? What a crock!

I leaned on my elbow, chin in hand, curiously perus-
ing the jury as the foreman got up to read the verdict of
"not guilty," and was shocked to feel my stomach give a
small lurch of disapproval. The man was guilty as hell,
he ran a disgusting business that shouldn't be tolerated
anywhere in our fair city, and it was my forked tongue
that had gotten him off. The girl stifled a sob, turned
over her chair, and ran heavily from the courtroom.

Percy turned to me and got me in a pretty tight bear
hug; I pushed him aside and spent a good fifteen minutes looking for the fat girl, but she had apparently fled
the halls of justice. I have no idea why I looked for her; I
think it was to apologize for my part in her undoing—
the thought kept running through my brain: What the
hell would such a misfit do now? God knows, no one I
knew would hire her. I had a momentary pang: Was I
turning into a softie, a knight with tarnished armor?

"McQuade," I told myself all the way back to
B. W. & M., "buck up. You got a nice fat fee, another
handy victory for the firm, and probably a commenda-
tion for excellence from old Mr. B. himself. Go home,
pour yourself an extra dry martini, and forget it."

But for some reason I couldn't. I got to my office on
the seventeenth floor of the black-glass Bank of
America building, looked out over the city I had grown
to love a great deal in the seven years I had been living

in it, and frowned. Had I been so successful because it is easy to be in such a magnificent and graceful city? City of lights. Or did the city seem magnificent to me because in my head it had begun to symbolize my success? God, it was a sight to behold at dusk, fog lifted, lights beginning to twinkle here and there! Perhaps the time had come for me to discover if this city really was "my lady" after all. Slowly, I turned to my desk and started emptying out drawers. I called my secretary, a pretty little piece with gorgeous tits and a tight ass, and asked her to find me a couple of brown supermarket boxes. She didn't even sound surprised. "Yes, sir," she chirped as she swung off. Within minutes she was in and out of my office, boxes deposited on the desk, kiss on my lips for congratulations on case won, and tilting walk out the door.

It took a good half hour to pack everything away. I left a year's supply of the *Law Review* in a neat pile in front of the antique bookcase I had bought at an auction in Bolinas some years back, as well as my law books and sundry other heavy items. The rest fit nicely into two supermarket boxes. I left my files for the good of the firm.

I sat down on my fine oak swivel chair and dialed out. "Margie? Mac here. You still want to sell the boat?"

I could picture her putting her hand over the mouthpiece and calling her husband Tim over in a hoarse whisper for a conference.

I had met Tim and Margie several months before when my friend Hunter and I had gone slumming in Sausalito. He was considering buying this beautiful catamaran that was moored next to an old thirty-eight-foot Kettenberg sloop called *Bessie*. She was owned by Tim and Margie. They saw us eyeing the boat next door, the four of us got to talking, and before long they had talked Hunter out of the catamaran. Tim knew of a better and cheaper one, moored in a marina farther north. Then we toasted Margie's pregnancy, verified several days before, with a bottle of white wine rescued from the depths of the trunk of my Jag. The young mother-to-be wanted to move to a "real house," but Tim wanted to stay put and was even hacking out a space for the kid in the quarter berth under the cockpit. He tended bar part time, "for necessary bread," but was a graduate of Stanford. Neither of us really understood Tim's lack of ambition. "Goddamned waste of a good mind," as Hunter put it. I said it was his life and he had to live it. The boat farther north was indeed a better buy. Hunter sent the young couple a basket of fresh fruit and gourmet cheeses, but we never saw Tim or Margie again. As far as I knew, they still hadn't resolved their quarrel and were still on the boat.

"Yeah, Mac, I guess we do. The baby's due pretty soon now . . ."

"Would it be a drag for you to move out this weekend?"

Thoughtful as ever.

Another quick conference.

"No. Actually, I'd even move today."

Tim got on the line. "You know of any cheap houses for rent anyplace in the Bay Area, Mac?"

I told them I was sorry that I didn't but suggested

they call a friend of mine who might. Tim thanked me; I guess he was tired of trying to persuade Margie to stay. Maybe she had persuaded him that a boat wouldn't make an ideal bassinet anyway. The deal was consummated in a couple of minutes. Tim suggested I drop by with the check that evening; they would try to move off the boat the next day. I was beginning to feel terrific.

I had a place to move to. It was a weird choice for me to be making, but I think it was the strangeness of the choice itself that was giving me the high. For the first time in months—God, it had been months—I felt a jolt of elation. To hell with those last few nagging doubts.

Sure, I like my creature comforts and have very expensive habits that are ill-suited to life aboard a sinking sloop! But I can give up the nine-hundred-dollar-a-month pad, the Jag—hell, everyone knows how much the upkeep on them is—and the double-breasted tweeds with matching vests, all purchased at Cable Car Clothiers, the soft cashmere jackets with velvet elbows from Dunhill's, as well as the fifty-odd shirts from I. Magnin. When I'm set up on the boat I won't need to keep several sets at the office for quick changes. To hell with my image. Whatever was happening to me was more than a momentary aberration. I had a feeling it was going to be a blast.

I moved to make it permanent and put in a call to the A. B. Peasley Company, the conglomerate that functioned as my landlord. They owned several large buildings on the Hill, mine included. I asked to speak to the office manager. We had a working relationship.

"Hi, Jack. Mac here . . . Yeah, thanks. It was an easy case. Cut and dried . . ." Suddenly I felt the need to get things settled fast. "Look, I hate to bother you, but I'm moving out over the weekend. No, nothing's wrong with the place; it's time for a change of scene, that's all. Albert's been after my pad for a long time. Give him a call; I'm sure he'll bite. Send me a check for the security at the end of the month, minus the days you lose. Maybe he'll move in over the weekend. What? Oh. Send it to me in care of the marina in Sausalito."

I waited for his wisecrack.

"Yeah, I found a great new chick over there. She's a real looker—name's Bessie."

Why bother explaining? Hell, I couldn't have, even if I'd wanted to.

I set down the receiver and began to thumb through the yellow pages. I dialed again.

"Hellow, Red Ball Moving? I'd like to move some stuff from the city over to Sausalito tomorrow sometime. What can you do for me?"

Whoever I was speaking to put me on hold, and then another tough butted in. He wanted to know what I had to move. I had been itemizing on my pad, so I had a pretty good idea of what was going. I read off the list; there was silence at the other end.

"That all you got, buddy?"

"No, but that's all I'm moving. How about it?"

The voice informed me the minimum fee was five hundred dollars. Then I started to bargain. I suggested he come and take a look at the four rooms of very expensive antiques I wasn't moving. He could have all of it for a thousand dollars plus the move. After a bit of haggling back and forth, he agreed.

"We'll be there between ten and two. You better be

35

home, buddy. And that furniture of yours better be as good as you say it is, or you're in a lot of trouble."

We hung up and I poured myself a martini, the first of the afternoon. It might be fun to be a bum for a while. I had been the hotshot "kid" lawyer for seven years and the thrill was wearing thin. Maybe I'd take some courses, move to Japan, or go into corporate law. It was, indeed, time for a change.

I buzzed Swivel Hips.

"Call upstairs to Mr. B., doll, and see if he has any free time this afternoon."

Her voice got all soft and purry.

"Anything wrong, Mac?"

"No, Shirley. Just give a buzz to Mr. B. like a good little girl."

Within seconds she was buzzing me back. Mr. B. would be free at four. Fifteen minutes. Fine. I went into my private washroom, took off my jacket, vest, and shirt, and soaped up. By five to four I was shaved and washed. I wanted to be on time that afternoon.

Mr. Barton's secretary was a washed-out, thirty-five-year-old spinster type who apparently swung in her free time. (I couldn't believe it, no matter how much office gossip I heard.) She kept her eyes to the ground as she ushered me in, and closed the door quietly behind her as she exited. No way, I thought to myself. The lady can't even look a man in the eye!

"Sit down, son," the old man rumbled at me from the depths of his deep brown leather chair. His chin was tucked into his shirt collar, his jowls hanging over in huge folds. He looked half asleep, but his twinkling blue eyes told the tale. He and my father had been classmates at Harvard Law way back when, and when I made the bar (also out of Harvard Law), it was assumed I would join his firm. All it took was one phone call from my mom.

Pops had died the preceding year from a heart attack, in a taxi on the way home from winning a very important and controversial case. He left my mother pretty well off and me a trust that I couldn't get my hands on until I was forty. I suppose he figured that I should make it on my own and that if I hadn't by the time I hit forty, I would need his money. For emotional reasons of my own I had never wanted to join my father's firm, so mom made the call to Barton in San Francisco. I was out on the Coast in two weeks. Two years later I had been made a junior partner, and last year I became a full-fledged senior partner. I was good: young, hot, handsome, and a headline-getter. Barton, Wells and McDonough needed me.

I sat down in the chair offered, stretched out my legs, and looked the old man in the eye.

A smile seemed to emerge from his jowls. "What can I do for you, my boy?"

I said it as straight as I knew how. "I'm quitting, Mr. B."

He didn't bat an eyelash, merely stared at me.

"I've had enough for a while. Thought I'd try retiring. Do some studying, see the Orient . . ."

Alf Barton gripped the arms of his chair with two thick paws and drew himself up. He cleared his throat.

"What about a three-month's leave?"

"Nope. That would be hedging my bets."

He pushed a button on his desk. "Evelyn, bring me Mac's file."

She whirred in and out, depositing a rather thick manila envelope on his desk. He leafed through the papers and only frowned once.

"According to the terms set forth, you have to sell us back your shares in the company." He looked up and I nodded. "You don't get any retirement to speak of, Mac. You're too young." Again he looked up, and again I nodded. He leaned back, folder in hand. "When do you want out?"

"Today."

His eyebrows went up an eighth of an inch. "I'm going to miss you, Mac. You're a good lawyer. Impetuous, but good. A real prodder." He sat there frowning into his collar. "Don't know that I'd be able to do much if you wanted back in, son. Bill and Jim'll be pretty upset about this. They won't understand it a'tall."

"I know that. That's why I came to you."

"Thought of doing the same thing myself, over forty years ago. I had a reputation, as they say. Could've gone anyplace. But Jocelyn was pregnant with Lucy, and Jaime was two. Always wondered what it would've been like if I had been single."

He pushed himself up and made it over to the bar. He poured himself Chivas Regal and made me a dry martini. He buzzed Evelyn and in she came. Without any ado, Alf told her to type up a set of retirement papers for me, following the proper procedure. She blinked, her ears moved, and a slow pink crept up her cheeks. Then she looked down, turned, exited, and set to work. We drank without saying a word. The click of Evelyn's typewriter could be heard through the thick oak door.

In a couple of minutes she knocked and brought in the papers. I signed, he signed, and Evelyn took them out to file. The old man and I shook hands, and I turned to go.

"Mac. Keep in touch. Jocelyn'll be mighty upset if you stop coming around right away."

"I'll be over for Sunday brunch." I opened the door and turned to add, "If you need me, contact the marina in Sausalito." I left the old man standing in the middle of his office with a sad, bemused expression on his otherwise expressionless face. I had the odd feeling he wished he were me.

Within minutes I had picked up my two boxes, told Shirley to transfer all my calls to Mr. B., and left. Shirley didn't know what to make of it, and I didn't lighten her load by letting her in on my imminent departure from Barton, Wells and McDonough. My Jag was in the usual place; I got in and sat for a minute, and then I started to smile. Broadly. Swinging into gear, I pushed off.

The Honda place was only about a mile away, so I made it there in seconds. Parking on the street, I went inside. It took only a few minutes to choose the make, a Honda 500, not too big but powerful enough to make it up those San Francisco hills and around the winding curves out to Marin. I pulled out my checkbook and looked right into the face of the chubby-cheeked, curly-haired salesman.

"I'd like to make a trade-in."

"Sure thing, what're we trading in today?" The grin plastered across his puffy cheeks.

"Jaguar. XKE, 1971."

The dumb-dumb's face hung open. He tried to close it and his Adam's apple bobbed up and down twice.

"Uh, well, sir. Uh . . . Well! Will you excuse me?"

He almost knocked over his chair as he turned to run to the manager's office. Moments later he returned, balding, thin little manager in tow.

"Well, sir." Baldie smiled at me, unperturbed. "This is a rather unusual offer. We can give you the cash for five Hondas, plus the one you're buying, in exchange for the Jag."

"Fine." I put away my checkbook and they took out theirs. Moments later, I was strapping my boxes onto the back of my new Honda. It felt real good. The drama was heightening.

For once I had no trouble parking. Ed, the doorman, gave me a funny look. I hit him hard on the back and gave him a big hello. I flirted with the little old lady who was hugging the wall of the elevator in order to give her poodle more room, and probably made her day, or week, or year. She was nearing seventy but wore lipstick and shadow whenever she stepped outside her door, even if she was merely going down to the laundry room. Sometimes she wore white gloves to walk the animal. My heart soared for a good deed done; she was smiling and nodding by the time we hit my floor.

First stop was my bathroom, where I opened up the taps, letting the warm water bubble into my specially ordered tub. Then I mixed up a batch of extradrys and poured the first. I took off my tie, jacket, and shirt, loosened my belt, and heaved myself into the black leather lounge chair. I picked up the phone, but Hunter wasn't home yet. Leaning back, I sipped with eyes closed. The only sound was the bath water, gushing into the tub. When the sound was right, I got up and turned off the tap. Then I tried Hunter again.

"Mac here. You still want the Eames chair, old man? . . . No, I'm not selling, I'm giving, you stingy bastard. Come and get it tomorrow, before two. See you then."

I rang off, grinning like a clown at the thought of Hunter's puss when he got to my empty pad. Hunter was an old chum from Yale, who was now the president of a large and successful bank in San Francisco. He loved his possessions almost as much as I did, and we both knew it. Good old Jess wouldn't know what hit him and would probably fear for my sanity. I'd tell him I was really okay. It was my decision and mine alone, and if I had screwed up too badly by leaving the hallowed halls of B. W. & M., and Japan didn't pan out, he could give me a job in his bank.

Before I got in the tub, I called Maryanne and told her to be ready at eight. We would sup at the Blue Fox and catch a flick at the old movie house in Ghirardelli Square afterward. I neglected to mention my change of vehicle. Let her make do.

By the time I hit the street in my warm Irish sweater and tweed sports jacket, I was polluted. It was a miracle I got to Maryanne's at all. She was standing in her vestibule, a petite little blonde in a long dress and big cape.

Her eyes almost bugged out of her head when she saw me swing into view. She came outside.

"You son of a bitch."

That's what I like, a sweet-talking woman.

She turned and was gone. Five minutes later, she was back in tight jeans—ironed, of course—Pucci blouse, and heavy sweater. The only reason the maître d' seated us was that I gave him a five-spot. Having been a steady Fox customer for seven years made no difference whatsoever. We were not properly attired clientele.

After eating, we got on the bike and zoomed up and down some hills for half an hour, out to Sausalito to deposit the check, and then, by mutual consent, stopped off at Maryanne's place. Maryanne is quite a piece. Tiny but lush, she has the ripe kind of build just right for whatever you've got on your mind. She enjoys her work, running a dress boutique in the Cannery, but she likes to play even more. We sat down for a very serious game of strip poker. It took me only two hours to win. I bedded her right on the living room rug, and by the end she was howling with pleasure. It began as a small gurgle in the depths of her gorgeous throat, turned into a growl—oh Mac, oh Mac, oh Mac—then she started to yowl. Her body gyrated me into spasms I would remember for a long time to come. Maryanne was no prude. She kissed me on the ear, murmuring my name again; then we both lay still. At four, I disentangled myself and tiptoed out. I had to get home to pack.

By twelve thirty, all the stuff I was taking with me was in the Red Ball van, and they were loading the antiques into the storage truck. The boss seemed pleased by my collection. He should have been. When Hunter arrived at two, the place was barren except for the Eames chair.

"What the hell's going on, old man?" He stared at me and then made his startled way from room to room.

"Thought I'd try out a boat in Sausalito for a while. I bought one last night. No sense owning something you're not going to use, don't you think?"

Hunter raised an eyebrow. "You're going to live in Sausalito?"

"Yup."

"I'll give you back the chair when you change your mind."

He snapped his fingers and Ivar, his former butler, hefted the thing to his shoulder and struggled out the door.

He was being very cool. As he was exiting, Hunter asked, "What's your number out there, old man?"

"I don't have one; I didn't order a phone."

"You're slipping, old man, you're slipping." He looked me up and down with that worried-old-lady look he puts on from time to time, shook his head, and left.

I made the necessary arrangements for a phone and was out at the boat before the movers. The couple was gone; all that remained was a cutesy note about leaving me cheese and wine to break the boat in with. They were nice kids. The place was immaculate, so I didn't have to use the Spic and Span or muscle I had brought along for the ride. I sat on the railing to await the guys from Red Ball.

A tall, thin brunette with a tousle of curls and legs up to her ass appeared on the next prow.

"Hi. You the new owner?"

"Um h'mm. The name's McQuade. Who're you?"

"Michelle. I live here with Buz when he's not on a bender."

"What do you do when he is?"

She grinned up at me. "I move around."

I was beginning to think I might like living on *Bessie*. She had no tits, but her legs more than made up for the lack. And what a mouth. Curved and pink, tip of the tongue just showing. I was turning into a real lech. The kid couldn't have been more than nineteen.

"What's the matter, Mac? You afraid of going to jail for stat?"

She was a mind reader, too. I grinned over at her. "Nope. But in my circle, the men do the propositioning."

She looked puzzled. "You must lose a lot of tail that way."

Then she ducked below deck. "See you later." She winked as she went under.

Red Ball arrived seconds later and was unloaded in half an hour. I played around with the furniture for a couple of hours, satisfied with the way things shaped up, and took a hot, hot shower. The head was fantastic. Those kids must have done a lot of groping in there. The tub in the foot of the shower was deeper than the usual model, deep enough for an adult to sit waist-high in water, and the shower had a movable nozzle so you could squirt yourself, or someone else, anyplace you chose. Very nice.

I was belting up my robe when I heard footsteps coming down the companionway, two light, two heavy. Michelle appeared in a long diaphanous thing and settled herself on my rya rug, which fit nicely in the compact but comfortable main salon behind the galley. I had left the berths on either side of the hull intact as well as the pull-out table for eating in the center. She was followed in by a big-looking bruiser with a surprisingly gentle face.

He outstretched a paw with a bottle of Scotch in it and said, "Welcome to the club, man."

I got out three shot glasses, but Michelle shook her head. She asked for carrot juice and went into the galley to look around. Buz and I downed ours and I put our second round on ice. Buz told me he did carpentry when he was sober and slept when he wasn't. He looked around at the raised Vitagenic I had installed in the double berth beyond the head in the bow of the boat and whistled in appreciation. We talked about the kind of shelves I could install underneath, including a dowel for hanging my shirts on. He held out his glass for more and I raised my brow.

"Michelle models for bread and fucks like a bunny for fun. But I'm soused half the time, so I can't blame her."

"Why do you drink?"

He grinned at me. "'Cause I like it."

"Touché."

"What do you do, man?"

I started to say I worked for Barton but thought better of it. In these circles that would seem square. Christ!

A fucked-up looker who screwed around, and another wastrel who hung out instead of working, and I was worried about appearances. What a mess people made of their lives. Still, I played down my former success. I had hit the front page of the *Chronicle* twice, and the second section often enough to be recognized walking down Sacramento, but I was pretty sure these two didn't read newspapers and therefore wouldn't be any the wiser.

"I don't know. I think I'm taking a breather. I used to be a lawyer."

"No shit. We could use a dude like you around here. They're trying to kick us all out of the marina. Close the place down; turn it into a fancy harbor for rich yacht-club types."

Like me and my friends. Buz didn't seem to notice my lack of response.

He took a healthy swig and held out his glass for more.

"We bring down the value of the water around here or something."

Michelle bounced up from the floor. "Come on, man. Don't bug the dude on his first night out. Let's go dancing." She turned to me with a leer. "You wanta come?"

"He's not bothering me, Michelle. And I don't want to come. It's been a long day."

I held out my hand to him. The girl's style was blatant and I pitied the guy. "Good to talk to you. I'll see you around."

He shook my hand and punched me on the back. "Thanks, man. Come on, girl. Let's move it."

46

And they were off, leaving me in my new boat, with nothing ahead and nothing planned. My steak came out rare, the potato tasted superb with sour cream and chives, the ice cream I had picked up in the square on the way over was perfect. I had two man-sized servings and hit the hay a full and happy man.

ANTONIA
3.

CHRISTOPHER AND I HAD A LOVELY LUNCH on Wednesday—we bought sandwiches at the caf but ate outside on the grass. Hesitantly, I agreed to meet him twice a week to eat, when our schedules converged. I also promised to go out with him that night, although I made it pretty clear I didn't want to rush things. As we stood up to go our respective ways, Christopher asked me if he could come to Rachie's birthday party.

"She sounds like a wonderful child; I'd love to meet her."

I paused in confusion; she *is* a handful, and I didn't want to scare Christopher away before I even got a chance to find out whether I wanted to get to know him. He misunderstood my dilemma completely.

"For Christ's sake, Tony, I'm not going to turn you in if I find out where you live. Stop being paranoid."

I shrugged, figuring "what the hell," and wrote our address and apartment number on his loose-leaf pad. I told him he might as well pick me up that night since he now knew where we lived. As I turned to go, I added, "That way I'll have more time with Rachie before she goes to bed."

Christopher took me to the Spaghetti Factory in San Francisco for dinner; we had a leisurely meal with wine, salad, and good conversation—the kind you have when you're getting to know someone you know you are going to like a lot. Christopher had gone to Swarthmore; he was four years ahead of me. So he already had his doctorate and was teaching at Berkeley.

"Christ, I love to teach. Kids at Berkeley are so bright and articulate."

Christopher's eyes sparkled when he spoke about his teaching. He was most inspiring. If I could get past my difficulty with Warren, I knew I'd feel the same way. Especially since the only enjoyable thing about school was my Marx tutorial. Some of the freshmen in Warren's Russian history survey course had never read Marx, so he and I decided I should offer an extra section on Marx so the kids would be able to understand Lenin, Trotsky, and Stalin, and their political differences, when Warren got to them. The seven freshmen still in the group had enough excitement about what they were learning to be creative. Maybe some would break through the system of "fall in line" and would stay that way, like Christopher.

"I especially love the first-year students. They're willing to try almost anything. I never stand up in the front of the room and lecture to them. Or at them. You know, this guy I did graduate work with has done a study about how important a simple thing like the placement of chairs is in a learning situation. Kids feel the freest when they're in a circle or on the floor, and when they feel free they contribute. That, in turn, increases the learning potential because ideas pass freely back and forth. Kids sure as hell learn more that way than they do taking notes.

"Jesus. I've been talking about my teaching for over an hour and that isn't what I wanted to do at all."

He looked at me very closely before continuing.

"Tony, are you still involved with Michael?"

I couldn't keep from smiling at the question, and how late in the evening it had come.

"No, Christopher. We haven't seen each other for over a year. I'm just annoyed with him for not coming around to see his daughter. You'd think he'd want to, but I guess he's given us both up for his new life. . . . No, we're not involved. I can't even believe we ever were."

He paid the check and we walked around North Beach, looking for a movie to go to.

"Why were you?" he continued to probe. Professors like asking questions.

"I guess because I wouldn't go to bed with him without that ring, and he never pushed me very hard. I was a 'good' girl. My God, we were naïve."

Simultaneously, we turned toward each other and stared. My legs began to tremble.

"Tony, would I get you home too late if we skipped the movie?"

"What time is it?"

"Ten."

"Yes, but Rachie'll be asleep and I can handle being tired tomorrow."

It was a miracle we ever reached his apartment, because Christopher kept turning to look at me all the way there. We only missed one turn off on the freeway. Then we made love on his living room rug because we didn't want to waste time traveling to his bedroom. His rug had a very soft shag; it was exciting to do it like that.

He insisted on walking me home. I was in the door by twelve, delighted with the evening, and surprised as well as pleased by Christopher's suggestion that he come over early Friday to help set up the decorations for Rachel's birthday party.

It was a big success; Christopher liked Rachie, but she wasn't so sure about him. He brought her an educational puzzle, but she preferred feeding breakfast to her two enormous rag dolls, and I could tell he was hurt. Even so, he couldn't seem to shed the role of teacher and play house with her. I figured they'd get used to each other by the time I finished icing the cake and they had blown up all the balloons.

Six kids came over; and Jeffrey, and Tom and Leslie (they have no children yet, and Rachie serves as their surrogate), Wendy, and Mrs. Guerin, the super's wife, who sits for us occasionally. Rachie calls her gramma.

Rachel got some wonderful presents—her favorite was another huge rag doll that was almost as big as she was. I cut a piece of cake and she fed it lunch immediately. The kids sat in a cluster around Rachel; one squealed in delight when he saw the books, another grabbed the doll, and a third raced around the room with a toy horse. Even the adults caught the enthusiasm of the kids. Rachie was in seventh heaven by the time she passed out the favors I had bought for each of the other children, and there was yelling and screaming as the little gifts were unveiled. We all ate the potato salad and franks, then Rachie blew out her candles and we polished off the cake as well. The kids went outside to get muddy, and we adults proceeded to consume the bottle of wine Christopher had brought over in the morning.

I carried the high from the party for several days until the morning I missed a bus and was late dropping Rachel at day care. I was rushing off to teach my first dance class when Wendy accosted me in the hall.

"Tony, we've got to talk."

"I know, Wend, I'm really sorry. I've just been so busy with papers and grading and all that shit . . ."

"Tony, I can't keep carrying Rachel. You owe me for August, September, and October. And November's payment's due in two weeks."

"Wendy! You've got to keep Rachel. What'll I do with her if I can't keep her here? I don't have anybody else in Berkeley I can leave her with when I go to class." I felt the knot on my neck tighten up.

"I know, Tony. But I've got bills to pay; I can't meet

the rent payment this month. I'm borrowing from Sally."

Sally was Marius's mother, and her husband, Tim, was a full professor, so they could afford it. At that moment my concern was for me and mine, as selfish as that may sound.

"Look, I'm late for class already. Can I call you tonight?" I was very close to tears.

"Of course. Oh, Tony. I'm sorry. But I don't know what else to do. I'm going to have to fill her place with someone who can pay."

"Tomorrow?" I almost shrieked the question.

"No, no, of course not. Next month, if I have to. I'll carry her until the first of December."

Mutely, I shook my head.

She continued, "You can pay me for all four months, then. That'll give you five weeks, okay?"

"What if I pay you off a little bit each month?" I held my breath, hoping. Wendy shook her head.

"I'm sorry, Tony, but I can't do that. Timmy's mother asked me a couple of months ago, and I said no to her, too. I just have too many bills."

I told her I'd find some way and left. What else could I do?

All the way to class I felt like I couldn't breathe. If Wendy wouldn't keep her those few hours every day, I would have to drop out of graduate school and get a temporary job. I had been hoping Wendy could hold off a few more months until I could build up a reserve from my classes and pay her with it, but that was apparently out. Christ, I was doing everything I could and it still wasn't enough!

By the time I changed and got to the dance room, my six little pupils were sitting quietly on the floor facing the mirrors, waiting for me to arrive. One girl had dropped out; she was a tubalina and couldn't take all the sweating that went into each class. The kids who remained were actually a very pleasant batch. My mind was really elsewhere, occupied with my plight, I suppose, but they were polite and full of admiration for me, and God knows I sorely needed some admiration in those trying times. First I worked the kids out sitting down, doing the exercises along with them. I concentrated on rhythm patterns going across the floor, and by the end of the hour the girls were laughing while they moved. As I was leaving the room, one of my favorite kids, a California towhead whose mother was a sculptress, grabbed me by the arm.

"Tony, I can't pay you because no one bought any of my mother's work this week, so we don't have enough. Should I drop out of class for a while?"

This was the worst possible day for her to drop that kind of bomb, but the poor kid couldn't help it. Neither could her mother. I sighed and told her not to drop out.

"Just pay me as soon as you can, Sally. I really need the bread."

She hugged me with gratitude and told me I was the first of their creditors that they'd pay. She was a very bright little eight-year-old.

By the time I hit my office, I was in a foul mood. There was absolutely no solution to my problems. Suddenly, dance classes were bringing in only $10 a week, Wendy was hounding me for $320 (which she certainly had a right to), and I had no other apparent source of income. I sat down at my desk, took out paper and pencil, and started to make up a list of possibilities. There had to be some way out. After all, I was a responsible, capable adult. All I needed was a little organization.

1. Drop out of school and get a job; keep Rachel at Wendy's full time.

2. Go on welfare—that seemed like a sound idea. With my income and family needs, I was sure I'd qualify.

3. Food stamps—ditto about qualifying.

4. Work for Wendy one day a week to pay for the other four days and arrange my class schedule accordingly.

5. A loan from my parents?

6. Locate Michael and get some money from him.

I felt very uneasy as I looked down my list. Number one. With only a B.A. in English, I knew I wouldn't qualify for much of anything jobwise: the job I would get would probably be as secretary, or editorial assistant, or proofreader, or something like that for $125 a week. Hours: 8:00 to 5:30. Rachel would never see me, so that seemed like a lousy solution.

This may sound old fashioned, but I believe very strongly that a young child needs to be with his or her mother a lot of the time. That was why I had decided to go to graduate school in the first place. My hours would be flexible there and Rachel would be at a day-care place three or four hours a day at most. More important, when I got my doctorate I could teach two or three classes and have the rest of my time free to play with my daughter. I could prepare for my classes and grade papers after she was in bed. My mother worked in my father's store when I was a kid and I never saw her. God, I was so lonely. I live in mortal terror of hurting my child in the same way. Number one was definitely out.

Number two. Now, welfare seemed like a real possibility. I called information and got the number but the line was busy for over an hour. I decided to call them the following morning, when I had more time. Ditto with number three.

Number four. Oh, shit. I suddenly remembered that Wendy had let her assistant go because she couldn't afford to pay her. Cross out four.

Five. Well, obviously my parents could be called only as a last resort. They would bring up Michael and his lack of support, try to make me miserable, and then plead poverty to get out of helping me themselves. I don't know why I even put five on the list.

Number six. Locate Michael. First, I put in a long-distance collect call to the Westleys—the blond couple Michael lived with in Wisconsin—but they weren't there. The girl who answered the phone said they were "in retreat" in the backwoods and were expected back in eight days. I told her I would call back but had little faith it would do any good. Michael lived on half of what we did.

Before depression set in I got organized and made up a little chart. Income went on one side, expenses on the other. The income side was very small. My fellowship gave me $233.33 a month, plus the $40.00 I earned from my dance classes. That brought the total up to $273.33. My rent was $135.00 a month for the one-bedroom place Michael and I had managed to find over five years ago. That was a plus. The identical apartment one floor below had had three tenants during my stay; the rent there was now $225! I slept on a couch in the living room. Food cost me about $35.00 a week, or $140.00 a month. I knew I could never cut back there, not with the rising cost of food. In addition, I was supposed to pay Wendy $20.00 a week. Jesus Christ. No wonder I was no longer making it. My monthly deficit came to $81.67, and would certainly increase as the year progressed, if I read my newspapers correctly on the state of the economy. Nevertheless, I still felt hopeful. Welfare and food stamps might just supplement me enough to compensate. Hell, it was the twentieth century. And who ever heard of a middle-class girl starving to death?

The next morning I called the welfare department, to see if we would qualify. After being referred to four different numbers, I finally found someone who would even talk to me. This is what I was told: a family of two with no income (presumably mother and child) is entitled to $197.00 a month on welfare. Since my fellowship gave me $233.33 a month, that let out welfare. The guy on the other end of the line told me to call the food stamp office. Their financial "scale" was different than welfare's.

I called food stamps. After several minutes of mumbo jumbo over the telephone, it became obvious that I would have to go over there. I went on Wednesday, and spent all morning waiting, and most of the afternoon filling out a three-page application, and talking to a caseworker. What surprised me was that the caseworker was young, with long blonde hair and an endearing smile: she looked like a lot of the kids I was teaching at Cal. As we talked, she did math like crazy, adding up three columns, dividing by nine, adding up some other numbers, and dividing again. I began to feel hopeful.

Then I tuned in to the conversation going on in the booth next door. One voice was gruff and male, the other, old, raspy, and female.

"You don't have any bank accounts?"

"No," came the quavering reply.

"When you had a savings account, what bank was it in?"

After hesitating a couple of minutes, the old lady mumbled, "I don't remember."

"What do you mean, you don't remember?" His voice got hard and loud. "Do you know what the penalty for lying is, lady?"

"Not all of the workers are like that, Ms. Weiner." My blonde student/worker touched my arm.

I couldn't keep from recoiling.

"Really! I'm sorry you had to hear that."

"You're sorry. What about that poor woman?"

My "worker" shrugged at me as if to ask, "What can I do?"; then she smiled so wide I could see her gums.

"You're gonna do okay. You qualify for sixty-one dol-

59

lars' worth of food stamps, and you'll only have to pay seventeen dollars a month for them!"

It was obvious from her response that I should have been ecstatic, but I wasn't. I had spent a whole day in this building that overflowed with old people, black women, and Chicano women, and listened to a lot of nastiness, only to discover that I would still have a monthly deficit of $37.67. According to the welfare department I wasn't poor; according to the food stamp people I was only entitled to a little bit of aid. I couldn't even grin and I knew that upset my worker. Her smile faded away and she reached out for my arm.

"It's better than nothing ..." Then she got more matter-of-fact, stick-to-business, and pulled back the arm.

"Call me in two months to set up an appointment so we can review your case. You'll have to come in every three months."

"And spend the whole day?" I blurted out before I could contain myself.

"No. We'll set up an appointment beforehand, so it should only take an hour or so."

I thanked her and stumbled out into the daylight. I stopped at the Café Mediterraneum to mull over my situation, and the guy behind the counter gave me a free espresso. He said I looked like I needed it. He was right.

So, welfare was out, and the money I would save with food stamps would only pay for two weeks at Wendy's Place, not more. If I continued with the dancing lessons, and none of my students dropped out, I wouldn't even break even. Where the money for Rachel's winter coat would come from was beyond me, let alone how I'd pay off my past debt to Wendy. And if a new emergency cropped up, I'd never survive it.

Well, that wasn't quite true. I would survive, because I was going to be resourceful. Tall buildings were beginning to seem shorter.

Okay, so it was dishonest. And unlike me. And scary as hell if I were to get caught. But. I could keep the same hours during the day and hire a sitter for the few hours a night, once or twice a month, I'd be out "working"— whatever it took to get enough money for us to survive.

Of course, I couldn't continue to rob Berkeley people. It would make me feel rotten and wouldn't get me all that much money, anyway, unless I went into the hills. The hills are patrolled pretty well by cops, so that didn't seem like a good idea. If I could get the names of some rich guys in San Francisco who headed up corporations that exploited Mexicans or South Americans or someone someplace, then I might be able to pull just a few big jobs and be done with it. No one would ever know, and Rachel and I could stop going through all this agony.

I approached Christopher indirectly.

"Christopher, one of Warren's students asked me how he could go about discovering who headed up some big, bad corporations in San Francisco, like Shell Oil, for instance, and finding out where they lived. I felt embarrassed telling him I didn't know, so I told him I'd get the list instead. How do I do it?"

"What's he going to do, kidnap them?"

I laughed. "No, he's going to mimeo it up and pass it out on the plaza. 'These monsters live in our midst,' etc., etc."

"Well, in that case, there are two books you can get in

the library. One is called *Manufacturers of California*; it lists the officers of all California firms. The other's entitled *Who's Who in the West*; it lists people, their jobs, and where they live. You could pick and choose from *Manufacturers* and then get the rest out of *Who's Who*."

"I like you more and more, Christopher. Do you mind if I never call you Chris and always call you Christopher?"

He took my hand in answer (he did know when not to talk!), and I was very sorry we were sitting in the school cafeteria, because my mouth was watering and tingling and so was every other imaginable place on my body. But there was nothing to be done about it. We played tag all the way across campus: he had a class to teach, and I had a daughter to pick up, so tag served as our cold shower. He asked me for a date for the following night and I suggested he come over for dinner instead. He agreed but only on the condition that he buy the groceries. He really did try to be considerate, especially at the beginning.

I told Wendy not to fill Rachie's place. I thought I'd have some money coming in from a part-time job within a few weeks. Maybe a month at the most. She said okay, as long as I paid her by December 1.

She looked very worried about her own decency, so I assured her I would get the money together in a month and that I understood why she had to ask for it. It was no lie; I did understand and was grateful she had carried me for as long as she had. I asked her if I could bring Rachel early the next day because I had some research to do in the library, and Wendy said, "Of course." She really was trying to be a good friend.

The night was cool but not cold, and very clear, so Rachie and I walked home, or, rather, I walked and Rachel skipped/ran/raced/hopped/twirled. She'd run ahead to the next corner and then turn around and make her way back to me, throw herself in my arms, and give me a hug and a very wet kiss. Rachel had scraped a bunch of skin off her stomach trying to climb off a ledge outside Wendy's Place, but it didn't seem to bother her. I told her Christopher was coming over for dinner the next night, and suddenly she looked downcast and worried.

"Will we have to feed him?" she asked timidly.

I had to fight back the tears as I told her that Christopher was bringing the food. She smiled immediately and twirled gaily into the foyer.

"Maybe he'll bring me a baseball this time," she called over her shoulder. We went upstairs, Rachie in my arms, clinging like a little monkey.

He didn't bring her a baseball but came equipped with Tinkertoys instead. Which went over fairly well, considering Rachel already had two sets, one from Michael when he was feeling beneficent, and one from my mother. Rach was very polite about it and I was very proud of her. Christopher would catch on eventually, I figured.

During dinner he taught Rachel how to play Botticelli and let her win over and over. He kept choosing things like *C* for Cookie Monster. Chalk one up for good old Christopher. If he was going to insist on intellectual games, at least he was willing to play them her way. We had spaghetti, Rach's favorite, and when she scolded Christopher for not buying the whole-wheat kind at Ma Revolution, he took it very well. She was adamant about my reading her a nighttime story; Christopher said he had papers to grade anyway, kissed me on the cheek, and left. Rach and I horsed around for an hour or so, and she fell asleep climbing on my back.

I found the books Christopher told me about immediately at the library the next morning and made a list of all the names I could have possibly used, with addresses, in about one hour. Oil company execs headed the list. I didn't think anyone would mind my robbing them. Heads of banks came next. Banks invest in South Africa and places like that, as everyone who knows anything is perfectly aware. Heads of rubber companies seemed almost as suspect to me because they exploit labor in South Africa. I didn't have to look further; that gave me plenty.

I started to walk across campus feeling very righteous about the whole thing when suddenly I stopped dead in my tracks with a momentary pang. What was I doing? What would my daughter say if she found out her own mother was becoming a criminal? What if I ended up in jail? Christ, the idea of jail hadn't even entered my mind. It just wasn't a place where I could end up, coming as I did from Short Hills, New Jersey.

Can you picture it? In the good old Antioch newsletter: "Antonia Weiner, class of '67, former graduate student at the University of California, Berkeley, is currently residing at San Quentin prison. She is doing ten years for grand larceny but should be out in time for her

64

high school's twentieth reunion. Anyone who would like to write to her or visit is welcome." Pretty absurd, isn't it?

Not only absurd but impossible. I couldn't get caught because I had responsibilities to my child. After all, she can't get along without me yet. Hell, what am I saying? I couldn't get along without her! Besides, I am the sort of person who could just never survive in jail.

Obviously, then, if I were serious about taking up burglary, I could never get caught. I would have to research how to do it, learn every nuance, and practice until I was sure I had everything down pat. First, I went to the library and took out two books on mountain climbing, one personal account of a burglary, and two Senate subcommittee investigations into crime. Then I decided to go to that huge army/navy store on Mission Street in San Francisco to find out about supplies, figuring no one would remember me at such a large place.

I arranged for Wendy to take Rachel home with her and bummed a ride into the city from Leslie and Tom, walking the few blocks from where they dropped me to the army/navy store. I looked around for a while by myself but couldn't make heads or tails of the ropes and prongs and pulleys assembled in the mountain-climbing section of the store. I went back to the counter and asked for some help.

"Hi. My boyfriend wants to take me mountain climbing and I've never been. I couldn't stand it if he knew I don't know anything about it, so could one of you guys explain it to me?"

They were aghast. Mountain climbing is not something you pick up in one easy lesson, apparently. Nevertheless, one of the older guys, with slicked-back curly hair, offered to help.

Loping to the back of the store, he rummaged around for a pad to sit on and then sat down on it himself. I braved it with the dusty floor. After all, I was going to be an outdoor girl.

First he took hold of the rope.

"You gotta always use nylon cording. Very light-weight and easy to handle. When I was a mountain ranger—I was a ranger in the Sierras back in '52—we used nylon at night so we wouldn't be heard by the animals we were stalking. It's nice and quiet."

I was getting a bonus I hadn't even asked for. I smiled prettily and got him to keep talking. Then he stood up and showed me how to wrap it around my butt, which he got a real kick out of doing, of course. He told me to roll the slack over my shoulder, letting it out as I needed it. He laid his big paw on my shoulder to illustrate the point.

"The boyfriend'll be real impressed. Want to try it?"

I stood up and did what he had done. It was pretty easy; the man was impressed by how agile I was. Then I asked him to explain the kind of hook I would be using. He said there was only one. It was three-pronged and called a grappling hook.

"Doesn't it make a lot of noise when it hooks into the rock, or tree, or whatever it hooks into?" I queried as innocently as possible.

"Oh, you can cover it with surgical tubing. It comes in a lot of thicknesses and one of them is bound to work. And you know, rubber is real adhesive, so it'll stick even better."

He explained how I would twirl the rope and heave it from down below if I was climbing up, as well as how to attach it firmly on the top if I was going down.

"I better getcha a pulley wheel in case you have to mountain hop. Your boyfriend'll be real impressed if you have one of those."

He showed me how to use it, braking with the handle every few inches as you swing across on the rope, but the whole thing was very nervous-making and I decided then and there I would always try to go down my buildings and not across. When I told him I thought I should get about a hundred feet of rope, his eyes bulged out of his head and he laughed.

"A little thing like you's gonna have a hell of a time lugging that much rope around. Nylon's light but not that light."

"That's what the Sierra Club manual says you need," I told him assuredly, listing one of the books I had gotten out of the library that morning.

"Sure, honey," he smiled at me condescendingly. "Anything your little heart desires."

I know what yours desires, I thought to myself. As for me, all I ask for is a few thousand dollars to see me through the next two years. I paid the man with the cash from two weeks of dance classes, leaving no telltale evidence behind, and hitched back to Berkeley. The man was right; the rope was heavy as hell. To carry the package, I had to walk all bent over from the weight.

I discovered over the next few days that I was quite relieved to have made my decision. First of all, it meant I wouldn't have to mess with food stamps if I didn't want to. I don't mean to sound spoiled or obnoxious, but have you ever had to shop with food stamps? Well, let me tell you, it is degrading and humiliating and embarrassing as hell. Rach and I went together—not to the Co-op, because I felt funny going someplace where people knew me, but to a small market in downtown Berkeley. We spent a good fifteen minutes picking out our supplies and got in line. When it came our turn, I pulled out the stamps and the cashier scowled. Meanly.

"The sign says Food Stamps Here. That means people with food stamps got to use that register!" She loaded up my cart again and sent us to the new line.

On the way over, Rach picked up one of those huge $1.25 Hershey bars. When it came time to pay, the new lady cashier looked at my daughter mournfully and put the candy back on the shelf.

"I'm sorry, honey. Mommy doesn't have enough money for that."

Now, I don't like Rach eating candy; but having that lady look at us like we were beggars really made me feel uncomfortable, so I scrounged up the $1.25, thinking the last time I bought one of these things it had cost 75 cents and that couldn't have been more than six months ago. Rach didn't understand the lady cashier but knew she had upset me. On the way home we both ate the candy. I worried about my next bout with food stamps. Now maybe there wouldn't have to be one.

Second, I was enjoying being with Rachie again because I knew I wouldn't have to give up any of my time with her. Third, I started to like my classes because I no longer felt pressure about whether I would be attending them the following semester. Suddenly, I was having less trouble with my little weekly and biweekly graduate papers; even I was impressed at my adjustment. I joined in the disgruntled discussions of my cellmates about the inequities of the scholarly system, gloating inwardly all the while about how I, in particular, was going to beat it all.

I worked extra hard in my dance classes, especially at the bar strengthening my arm muscles. Jeffrey was suitably impressed with my efforts and started bugging me in earnest to join his dance troop. "What's a nice girl like you studying Russian history for?" and dumb stuff like that.

When my parents called me on Sunday, they marveled at the timbre of my voice, at the chipper way I spoke about this and that. Finally, my mother inquired rather hesitantly (for her):

"Antonia, have you found a guy, a steady guy?"

"No, Ma, whatever gave you that idea?"

"Well, you sound so happy."

"For Christ's sake, there are other things to be happy about besides a man, Ma!"

"Like what?"

"Like . . . (*Long Pause*) like getting all good grades in school and being invited into Jeffrey's dance company." (Thinking in my mind, "Like robbing apartments by vaulting in over the roof and getting away with it.")

"But Antonia, Jeffrey is always inviting you into his company."

So what could I say? That was quite true. I dodged around the question for a few minutes and then tried to sound depressed over the phone. That seemed to make my mother happier. Then she could say, "I told you it wouldn't be easy, raising a child alone."

I spent the last week of October slowly going over my list of prospects, until I had narrowed it down to five: two bank presidents, the head of a big oil company, the president of an architectural firm that was destroying the beauty of old San Francisco, and a rather boring, single business executive (rubber).

I immediately discounted the head of the oil company when I discovered he had three daughters, aged eleven, fifteen, and nineteen. The comings and goings of the teenagers would be much too erratic to set any stock by. One of the bank execs was out of town on a honeymoon, so the maid informed me when I was doing my survey on how many people reside in old Victorian mansions in the Russian Hill area! And the head of the architectural firm had a sister and her two kids staying with him for a couple of weeks. The business executive was ugly and boring and rarely went out, so that left the other bank executive, who apparently envisioned himself a real stud. He had girls holding their breath all over the city.

His name was Jessup Hunter III, and he was more obnoxious than either his father or grandfather had been before him. A thirty-five-year-old bachelor, he visited his widowed mother on Thursday evenings for one hour and then came home (not enough time for what I had in mind, so that left out Thursdays), saw his various female friends five nights a week, and stayed home Sundays playing cards with the guys. Probably poker; he was the type. He was tall, dark (but Aryan), and attractive in a Burt Reynolds sort of way. He wore tight pants, to show himself off to best advantage, and flashy shirts. Nevertheless, he looked square; although given the number of girls he had or had had, my opinion seemed to be in the minority. None of this was in *Who's Who*, but *Time* had done a story on him in 1969. He was president of a bank notorious for its involvement in South Africa. Said bank was picketed for a while, but the picketers trickled away to other causes, and the bank continued doing evil things. To make matters worse, he was on the board of one international conglomerate that was well known for its exploitation of people all over the globe, including their workers right here in the good old U.S. of A. In addition, he was on the letterhead of this, and the masthead of that, and didn't belong to one good charitable institution. All of his excess money he put into his one and only passion besides women—antique African art (jewelry, statues, ceramics, and the like). According to *Time*, he had removed most of that from the country in which it belonged to bring it back to his rather modest, but ugly, apartment.

I went to the bank to see him for myself, and he was just as I had imagined. A prick. Very conceited, he oiled his way from female cashier to female cashier, giving the prettiest one a lovely little pinch on her rather large rump. The only time he stopped oiling about was when a business-exec type needed his advice. Then he got very precise about everything. He had lunch every day promptly at 12:35 at Poole's and returned to his office by 2:35. He left work at 5:00 and walked home to his modern, hideous apartment house. Good for the physique, I imagine. I followed him twice and it's a good thing I had my dance classes. Without them, Hunter's tour of the city would have laid me out flat on my back. His lights went on at 5:40. By 6:15, "Jess" could be observed on his balcony, sipping what looked like a dry martini. He went back into his living room, closing the balcony door behind him but never locking it. I know, because I watched him on two different occasions from the cocktail lounge of the Mark Hopkins Hotel.

The apartment itself looked better than the lobby. The first time I walked past the building I almost died. Trees with orange flowers, yellow flowers, and blue flowers—tall and imposing—stood just inside the lobby door, flanked by terribly thick and ugly, off-white "Mediterranean-style" furniture. The couches were patterned affairs in orange and aqua with a white background. It wasn't until I aimed my binoculars at Hunter's balcony that I realized the little orange and aqua things on the couches were exact replicas of the charming little-boy statues found on each of the balconies of each of the luxury apartments; only on the couches, some were little girls and some were boys. I never did find out if the little-boy statues sprayed water.

Anyway, luckily the other customers at the Hopkins took me for a tourist. Their lounge stays open late. Three nights I stayed glued to the window until they closed and took careful note that Hunter rarely returned home before 3:00 A.M. Rachie slept over at Nicole's house on those nights. When Hunter did return to his monstrously ugly apartment house, it was usually alone. So most likely he did his loving at the young ladies' apartments. Christopher was very uptight because I wasn't available very much, and I got very good at making excuses. It was my only choice—I certainly couldn't tell him what I was really up to.

After watching Hunter for two weeks, I had no doubt at all that he was a creature of exact habit and therefore would be a very easy fellow to rob. He was never home in the evenings (between seven and one in the morning), except for Thursdays and Sundays. I decided upon the Tuesday of the week before Thanksgiving because I wanted to be sure of being able to afford a turkey with all the trimmings on Wednesday.

All that remained was for me to become proficient with that rope gizmo. Which I did late at night, after Christopher had left and Rachie was long since in bed, along with everyone else in the immediate vicinity. I certainly didn't want to be observed by any of my neighbors.

I had only one mishap, and that was when I lost my footing because of the clumsy boating sneakers I was wearing. My body veered out over the hedge and I jumped down to the earth below. Then I threw up in the bushes. The next night I wore my ballet shoes, and for some reason they worked much better for me. They were lighter and I was used to the feel of them on my feet. I landed in my apartment every time, without even disturbing the sleep of my daughter, who is a light sleeper. Once, I even came in her window, just to make sure about my own agility. Had she awakened, I don't know how I would have explained myself. Thank God I never had to.

ANTONIA
4.

TUESDAY NIGHT I ARRIVED TEN MINUTES
late because there had been an accident on Van Ness and
the bus I was on couldn't get around it. I missed Hunter's departure, which made me slightly nervous, but I
had put too much into the evening to give up on it; I
went ahead as planned. My suitcase was waiting for me
in the maid's linen closet on the third floor of the Hopkins. I had found a closet that was never locked, in case
someone needed spare bedding after the maid went
home, I suppose. It was a schlepp, but I got the suitcase
across the street and started ringing doorbells at Hunter's place by seven. I figured someone would let me in

without having to hear me tell them who I was and why I was there. It took only three rings. I was up on the roof by 7:15. A water drainpipe was sticking up about four feet from the ledge of the roof, a little bit to the left of where I wanted to start down. It looked more promising up close than it had from my vantage point across the street. I looped the end of the rope around the pipe several times and then stuck the hook through to keep it in place. I tugged and tugged, and nothing came loose. Then I walked to the ledge, holding the rope over my shoulder, and hoisted myself up.

It was dark as hell; I couldn't see a thing at first. Then my eyes loosened up, and I looked down. My practicing had really paid off—I didn't even get slightly nauseous. I could just make out the outline of the three balconies leading the way to Hunter's place. His was four down from the top and had no canopy. The first apartment down had an escalloped one, in stripes, totally blocking my view of the ledge and floor. The second one down was bare and dark; no one was home. The third was partially hidden by a half canopy, very narrow, and I could see a light twinkling out into the night. It flickered and went out. What great luck—no one home there either.

I held my breath, closed my eyes, turned, squatted, and let myself down over the edge, very slowly and carefully, until I was crouched against the side of the building just under the ledge, feet pressing up against the wall. I felt very cramped. Hanging onto the taut part of the rope with one hand, I arched my back until my head was leaning over backwards, looking down at the street, and took in a couple of gulps of fresh night air. Then, abruptly, I pulled myself back into the crouch again and sat there for several minutes, suspended in the pitch black. I was too close to the side of the balconies; the canopies were in my way. Quickly, before I could get too scared, I flung out my hand, the one gripping the taut part of the rope, and moved it at least two feet farther to the right. Thank God, it worked! Slowly I began to creep down the building toward the first canopy.

It was very cold out, although luckily for me there was no wind, and I remember regretting that I hadn't worn a sweater. I had wanted to be as light as possible, so all I had on was my blue leotard and a pair of faded old jeans. Funny, I suddenly remembered it was the same outfit I had worn to rob Christopher.

When I reached the first canopy, I brushed it with the palm of my hand, to see when it ended, and continued on by to the balcony itself. I was tired, so I found myself lunging at the railing. I flung out an arm and made a grab for it, at the same time swinging my feet down and jumping to the floor of the balcony. I did a shallow knee bend to keep my balance as I landed, and straightened up slowly. I leaned my whole weight against the railing.

I knew I only had a couple of minutes to rest—and my Lamaze training from when Rachel was born came in really handy. When I rested, I really rested. In three minutes I was off.

I swung my feet out and up, held on tightly to the rope, and found myself crouching against the building to the right of the first railing. This time I didn't wait but started right down. It took me a good five minutes to reach the next canopy; I passed the open balcony without stopping because I wasn't that tired. What a mistake! I was about to swing my feet down to the cement floor of the balcony above Hunter's when the light flicked on in the living room beyond the balcony. Goddamn it, they were back. Suspended in motion, I sort of hung there for several seconds in midair, swinging from side to side. Jesus, I was terrified. I kept seeing Rachie asleep in bed all alone. My feet kicked in toward the building, but I couldn't get a good grip on it, so my kicking motions seemed futile and absurd. It was useless. I gave up trying to hug the building and began to let the rope out, swinging down the rest of the way to Hunter's place, like the pendulum in Poe's short story. The rope stopped several yards short of Hunter's railing. I only hung there a second before I jumped. My arms were numb and I had no choice.

I must say, all things considered, I landed magnificently, knees bent, only a foot away from a huge potted palm. I touched the leaves and was genuinely surprised. It was real. I did a couple of chaîné turns to disentangle myself from the rope and left it dangling. The night was clear, but it was awfully dark, so the outline of the rope wouldn't have been discernible against the building. I peered into the living room but it was dark, so I tugged at the balcony door and it came open easily.

My eyes were accustomed to the dark, so I didn't bother turning on a light. Besides, it felt safer that way. If anyone heard a noise and got curious, they'd take one look and be convinced that no one was home.

I admit I was quite surprised at what I found. Hunter

had exquisite taste in African jewelry; each little bauble was more beautifully detailed than the next. Considering the absolute hideousness of the building he lived in, this was most unexpected. I mean, I knew he'd have expensive stuff that I'd be able to hock easily, but I never thought I'd like any of it. After some deliberation, I chose two antique African statuettes (they turned out to be worth a small fortune—I chose them because they were small and light and fit into my canvas shoulder bag very easily), a silver necklace, bracelet, and earrings in their glass-enclosed case. On the table behind the white couch, I found a tiny jade pinky ring and couldn't resist slipping it on my right hand; it fit perfectly.

Then I realized I was starved; what the hell, Hunter wouldn't miss a little ice cream, if he had any. He did, chocolate, from Ghirardelli Square. I found a priceless antique spoon and gulped down several mouthfuls. When I had finished I wanted to wash and dry the spoon, but, afraid I had lost enough time already, I pocketed it instead, as well as a silver pie and cake cutter, a steak knife (a beautiful gold thing with lots of inlay work), and a set of corn holders (also gold).

I left the kitchen, very satisfied and greatly pleased with my booty. I toured the dining room but didn't take anything. I skipped over the Limoges china because it was breakable and heavy, and headed for the bedroom, where I hoped I'd find some spare change Hunter might have left lying around. On the way there, I passed a funny little room, lined with books (the second bedroom, I guess), and carefully went through the shelves. I took an original Dickens because I figured it might be worth quite a bit on the open market, an Elizabeth Bar-rett Browning, a thin volume of *Winnie-the-Pooh* for Rachel, and the copy of *Who's Who in the West* that listed Hunter. I did that because I knew it would drive the elitist crazy when he discovered it. All of them went into the canvas bag, which holds quite a lot, considering its small size.

Hunter's bedroom was a veritable gold mine. He kept a lovely little gold antique box on his dresser, which he filled with ten- and twenty-dollar bills. I counted out the money—$150—put it in my wallet, and stashed the box in the top of my canvas bag. It was pretty full; the flap barely made it across the top. But the little box was well worth it; I got $75 for it at a little antique shop off Polk several days later.

For some reason I didn't stop there but decided to check out the dresser, too. I carefully emptied each of Hunter's drawers, one at a time. I couldn't keep myself from neatly folding and replacing each item of clothing when I had finished with it. If he didn't check carefully, Hunter would never realize I had gone through them. I did it systematically, from top to bottom, left to right, and unearthed the door prize in a couple of minutes. Hunter hid a bundle of hundreds in a pair of socks in the back of his underwear drawer. It's a stupid place to hide anything, much less five hundred-dollar bills; the dumb schmuck. I bet he keeps his money in his bank now!

The only other thing I took was this marvelous little lamp Hunter had snapped to the headboard of his bed. It was stronger than a tensor (which I couldn't afford) and would really help me when I studied at night after Rachel was in bed. It headed my personal list of necessities and fit in the satchel with a minimum of rearranging, so in it went.

I let myself out the front door; no one was around. By the time I hit the elevator, I was smiling with relief. Which, as it turned out, was a big mistake.

First I went up to the roof, pulled up my line, and repacked the suitcase. I hauled it down the flight of stairs and rang for the elevator, panting from the effort of lugging the thing that far. There was no company waiting for me in the elevator, so I tried to compose myself on the trip down.

I don't know what I did wrong, where my planning went askew, but when the elevator opened up at L, there he was, standing there like he thought he was God's gift to women. Hunter. I was the only one in the elevator; when he saw me his male rat-eyes lit up, he pushed his hip up against the rubber part of the door, and leaned against the far wall with his other arm, thoroughly blocking my exit path. I almost died, but he didn't seem to notice anything other than my boobs.

"Well, hello!" He only paused briefly. "Why don't you let me carry that?" He reached for the canvas shoulder bag. "I'll give you a ride to your dance class."

Obviously, he took in the leotard and jeans, the hair in a bun at the nape of my neck (everything neat and tidy for my ascent), and decided *dancer*. I was having a lot of trouble breathing; but the way Hunter was taking in every inch of me made me so furious I almost forgot my terror.

"No, thanks," I said as loud as I could. It came out kind of squeaky. "You son of a bitch," I thought to myself.

The buzzer rang on the tenth floor, but he ignored it. "Let 'em wait. How about it, doll?"

This time my voice was stronger; he was making me mad.

"Would you mind? I'd rather not spend my entire evening in the elevator."

"Honey, if we could spend it together you wouldn't mind, would you? The name's Jessup Hunter III. What's yours?"

Hearing him say it so directly made me feel just weird. After all, I was standing there with half his apartment over my shoulder. I could feel the pink creeping up my neck and spotting my cheeks. He took it as acceptance and stood there salivating in anticipation. The buzzer rang again.

"My name's Eliot. The first name's George." I could tell by his face that he actually got it. "Excuse me," I tried again.

"You're cute, doll, but you don't know enough. George may have written under a pseudonym, but she was quite a gal. The way she carried on with Mr. Lewes shocked the pants off her mother, I hear."

"My mother doesn't shock so easily. But I do. Excuse me."

"Don't get your dander up. I could show you quite a time. Look," he lounged against the door with incredible insolence, "my date got the flu tonight, but you and I could still use the reservations I made at the Blue Fox. What do you say, doll?"

So that explained his early arrival. Well, at least it hadn't been my fuck-up. A little old WASP lady with a dog entered the lobby. The animal yapped at Hunter's heels, but he seemed unperturbed. Nothing whatsoever seemed to bother him or deter him from his planned course of action. I was getting very anxious and kept sticking my right hand behind my back. Damn that ring. I felt myself flailing about.

"I'm not dressed right."

He reached down at me and did something appalling: he tried to kiss me. Instinctively, I pushed him away with both hands, talking as I pushed.

"You're sensational, but I've got to go, doll. How about it?" He stepped back, clearly not used to being turned down.

"Okay, we'll call if a stand-off. You've got great taste in jewelry, lady," he added as he let me pass by.

My knees started to shake—What the hell did he mean by that?—but I made it to the lobby door. The suitcase felt like it was loaded down with bricks, which felt worse because I was trying to carry it with a straight back. What else could I have done? If he had realized how heavy it was, the schmuck would have probably demanded to carry it for me. I pulled open the door, realized I had made it, and pivoted for a parting shot.

"And you've got lousy style."

The dog barked furiously and the old biddy cackled, but I'll say this for him. Hunter managed to get in the last line before the elevator door closed him out.

"Suit yourself, doll."

I don't think I'll ever be able to get the sound of that phrase out of my ears. The bus ride home was uneventful. I paid Mrs. Guerin, looked in on Rach, stashed the canvas satchel in the back of my closet, and fell into bed. I was asleep in seconds.

I still wonder how long it took him to discover the little ring was his. . . .

McQUADE
5.

MY HEAD FELT LIKE STALE COTTON CANDY: I knew if I even touched it, fingertip to temple, it would crack down the center. It had been a hell of a Thanksgiving and wasn't quite over yet. Michelle had only left an hour before, and I wasn't at all anxious to haul my ass out of the large, superfirm Vitagenic I had shipped out to *Bessie*; there would be plenty of time for that later in the day. The world could buzz along without my help for one more morning. I rolled over and shoved the down pillow over my head and tried to go under one more time. The loud clang of the cowbell I'd rigged up topside interrupted my plans. The damned thing jangled loose whatever equilibrium I'd managed to maintain; my head was no longer throbbing—it pulsated, temple to temple.

I shuffled my feet over the edge and decided I couldn't stand the sound another minute. I yelled, top voice, "Shut up, you bastard, whoever you are. I'm coming." I made it to the companionway pretty quick, all things considered, and slid back the hatch, opening the shutters part way to admit as little light as possible. Even with my eyes half closed, I couldn't believe what I saw.

Jessup Hunter III lives by routine: he has run the same course for over ten years and only altered it once, when he was hospitalized for appendicitis in '65. Even then, he demanded that the nurse ring up Poole's to order him lunch at 12:15 every day, and she, of course, obliged, Hunter being who Hunter is. The hospital was peeved but eventually pacified. So. To find Hunter on my deck at 11:00 A.M. on a sunny, crisp winter day when he belonged in his bank at Montgomery and Market was totally shocking, even with my head feeling the way it was feeling. I tried my damnedest to be polite.

"Jesus Christ! What the hell are you doing here at eleven in the morning?"

"I brought coffee—black—and toasted English. I presumed you'd have eggs on board. May I?"

With his usual grace, Hunter pushed me aside and made his way to my galley. He set the little white bag on the counter top and moved into the salon, frowning at the big bed as his Gucci shoes caught on the only rug and catapulated him into pop's chair. He stayed put. Now, Hunter knows that chair has always been my territory, and territory is one thing we have always been very careful about. Something was definitely up, but playing the game we always play, I didn't even raise an eyebrow.

My initial outburst was taken as pique at being awakened so early and was ignored by both of us. His breaking training was pushed aside in my rush to be cool. I did my morning shuffle into the kitchen and uncapped the coffee before opening my mouth. It was awful: it came from the diner on the other side of the marina that I had vowed never to enter again, seeing as they were out to poison their clientele. I grinned, or tried to. My face felt miles away, like it was camping out at Disneyland, but I plodded on just the same.

"How about an omelet? I'll even throw in a little tarragon to make you more comfortable."

"You have any mushrooms?"

"Sure. No good sloop could ever be without."

Neither of us said a word until the omelet was on the pull-out table, and even then I was pretty casual.

"The bank take a legal holiday?"

"Nope." Hunter answered. "I took off a little early."

At that I raised my brows.

Before I continue, I think I should tell you a little bit about Hunter himself. The head of the San Francisco branch of a reputable bank by the time he was twenty-nine, Hunter seemed pompous for his years. To make matters worse, he sat on the boards of various prestigious conglomerates as well. He was about thirty-five— give or take a few years depending on whom you chose to believe, Hunter or his mother—graying at the temples, swarthy in a very Anglo-Saxon sort of way, tight-lipped, fastidious, and a bon vivant. He drank inordinate amounts, but never seemed drunk, and kept six or seven pretty little things dangling on his string from one month to the next. All hoped to inherit the heir apparent, I would guess, so they all hung in there. Or maybe he had found something new to do in bed that he hadn't told me about, and they were addicted and couldn't get out.

I must confess that once I tried to make a little time with one of Hunter's beauties; it was an abysmal failure. She let me take her to Amelio's, possibly the most expensive and chic place to dine out in my fair city, ordered frog's legs, steak au something, mousse, and a 1952 champagne. At the time I could afford it, so I didn't mind. I do now, knowing that she let me take her there with a full awareness of what was to come. Or, more precisely, what wasn't. We dined and walked about the city like lovers, and then I took her home. Where she turned around at the door, told me what a lovely time she had had, kissed me on the cheek, and slipped into her tiny vestibule. Luckily for me, she never told Hunter. I did, about two weeks later when the shock had just about worn off. He had a good laugh while I suffered in silence. Hunter can be a boor; he laughs loud and seems to hiccup between guffaws. As I silently listened to his nonsensical trumpet of victory, I vowed that I would make it up to him, somehow, somewhere, someday. I hoped it would be soon. Hunter brought me back to the present with a scowl.

"Don't be a wise ass today, McQuade. I'm not in the mood."

"What's up?"

"I was ripped off the night before last."

"No shit? I didn't think anyone could break security in that monstrosity."

He glared at me. "Don't knock the building, old boy. You lived in one just like it until last week."

"At least mine had real plants in the lobby and no statues on the balconies!"

Hunter mumbled something about art deco; but I said, "Bullshit. Ugly is ugly."

Besides, all of the apartments in his building are identical white boxes, differentiated only by the paintings their occupants choose to hang on the very thin and fake walls. Each two-bedroom lovely goes for a mere $1,050, the cost rising as the apartment itself rises. Those on the fifteenth floor cost a piddling $1,750. Whoever lives in them must be either blind or crazy.

Hunter's eyes never left my face. He continued talking right past my grinning puss. "I believe she found it quite easy."

No shit! A *she*. I couldn't help but feel delighted that one of Hunter's ladies had finally done him in. He was getting a little back and it served him right. I got up to clear the table.

"Which one did it? Dolores? No, Abbie has more guts."

"Shut up, McQuade. You look lousy; I know you had a rough night, so I wouldn't press it if I were you."

Being an okay guy, I resisted the impulse to say, "How can I help it?" and poured us each a cup of my home-brewed coffee. It's the one thing I'm still finicky about.

Aristocratic taste never quite dies, I suppose; besides, I know there is no substitute for good coffee. Taking some Cannery Danish out of the oven, I deftly dropped them center-table, grabbed the two coffees plus the cream, and sat down across from old square-jaw.

"I'll try, old man. Who is *she*?"

Hunter cut himself a slice of Danish and gulped down half a cup before answering.

"Look. This really isn't at all funny. I wasn't going to tell anyone, but I want the jade ring back."

"The one your grandmother gave you before she died?"

Hunter had a mouthful, so he merely shook his head. This was serious. Both Hunter and I really dug that old broad. At eighty-two, she remarried an old railroad man who had worked for Jessup Hunter I, as a porter. Old "Jess" had only been dead for two years when she married the "lowly," as he was referred to by her relatives, so it caused quite a sensation. One night, when Hunter and I had gone over to have some brandy with the newlyweds, Virginia proceeded to describe their wedding night. She wasn't at all shy about it. "You're never too old, son," she smiled as she took Hunter's hand. "And don't you ever forget it." As I said, Hunter and I both dug the old lady a lot. That evening, before we left, she gave each of us one of her rings. Heirlooms from the mother country, they were beautiful things. Hunter's was jade; I chose an opal. She made us promise we would keep them until we each found a "little lady worthy of having it placed on her precious pinky." Hunter exhibited his in a made-to-order glass case in his living room; I kept mine in a safe on the boat. The safe was well hidden. I knew that losing that ring was no laughing matter; having it ripped off, well, that was serious business.

"You sure it's gone, Jess? Maybe Ida moved it when she was dusting yesterday."

Ida was Hunter's Irish maid, who came in a couple of hours every day and never talked about what she had to clean up. Occasionally she'd look at me and shake her head sadly, but she never nagged at Hunter. Even though she had taken care of him since he was a "wee tot," he was a man now and what he did was his business.

"No. I called her and she got pretty pissed off. She said she knows where everything belongs better than I do. She's probably right."

Hunter looked very carefully at the piece of omelet he was about to consume. He was through talking.

"Hey, man, you being straight with me about all this?"

"What do you mean, McQuade? Of course I'm being straight."

But he wasn't. I've known Hunter ever since we raised hell together at Yale. I was actually studious my freshman year, but Hunter, one year ahead, quickly showed me the error of my ways. We caroused together for two and a half glorious years—it took half a year for me to unbend and stop cracking those books—and hit all the best spots: Holyoke, Wellesley, and our special favorite, the magnificent and stately old Sadie Lou. Known to poor schnooks from Dartmouth and Amherst as Sarah Lawrence, they never got to first base there. My God, what the sight of all those beautiful and lovely debutantes still does for my soul! It will never be so simple again.

Upon graduating, Hunter and I went our separate ways: me to Harvard Law School and Hunter into his father's bank. He took a graduate business course at Stanford and eventually got his degree. Very few people know Hunter is Dr. Jessup Hunter III; he thinks it sounds too stuffy. And, God knows, Jess is stuffy enough as it is. I think he must go to bed in a vest, although he denies it. Funny thing is, he denies that, just like he denied lying to me that morning aboard *Bessie*. The one thing I've learned about Jess through all these years, other than that he's a hell of a boozer, is that he's a lousy liar.

"Come on, Hunter, fess up. Something about this little tale doesn't ring true."

"Lay off, will you!" He looked at me, scowling.

Neither of us said anything.

"Okay. I think I know who she is."

"It *is* Abbie! So, what do you want me to do? Go over and rough her up a little bit?"

"It isn't Abbie, McQuade! Look, this is hard enough as it is. If you could just shut up for a minute, I might be able to get it out." That was a mouthful for old Hunter, so I clammed up. I left it up to him.

"Miranda got sick last night . . ."

"It was Miranda? I never thought she had that kind of moxie."

Hunter glared.

"Miranda got sick. But she didn't tell me until I had arrived at her place and found her spaced out and flat on her back. I slapped a wet washcloth on her forehead, gave her some hot tea, and got the hell out. I hate the flu."

Hunter sure was dragging this thing out. Maybe I was due for a good laugh after all.

"Suze was busy, and Abbie hates it if I call her at the last minute, so I walked home." He stopped and stared at his omelet again.

"Come on, man. Out with it or I'll go back to bed."

"Okay, okay. I got back to the building at eight something and rang for the elevator. I think the elevator was on nine. Anyway, it went up to fourteen, fifteen, and sixteen and came back down. The door opened and this girl was standing there. Jesus, McQuade, I thought I'd drop my pants right there. Knockout doesn't even begin to describe her."

He launched into a description, giving special attention to the nipples of her tits pressing up against the blue of her leotard top, and her thatch, which he swore he could see through her jeans, they were so tight. I've got to admit, my mouth watered a little, but I decided I'd let Hunter have her. He saw her first and he deserved her. After all, she had ripped him off, not me.

"I thought I was doing pretty well; she was blushing and looking down and doing all those things a chick does when she doesn't want to show she's interested."

Or so he thought before he got up to his place and discovered she had ripped him off. What he couldn't get over was that he had offered to carry her bag! His bag, really, if you considered what was inside it. But I'm jumping ahead. Hunter was just beginning to warm up to his story.

93

"I really think I might have made it, Mac, and saved her from a life of crime at the same time, if it hadn't been for that old busybody, Miss Pringle in 719. A few of us got a petition together last year to have her evicted, but she wouldn't move. The silly old fart had to come into the foyer at that particular moment, with her lousy rotten yapping dog. The poodle starts snapping at my ankles, the girl begins cooling off, and Pringle is listening, all attentive to every word."

I was beginning to catch on. "What you're trying to tell me is she got away."

He nodded his head.

I couldn't resist. "How the hell could you let a piece like that get away?"

"Fuck off, Mac!"

He slumped down and stared straight ahead. "I didn't realize anything was missing until I got into bed to read. She took my lamp, Mac, the one I special ordered at Abercrombie & Fitch. Why the hell would she do a thing like that?"

"You got me, Jess. What else'd she take?"

"The antique statuettes, a necklace, bracelet, silver spoon, those gold corn holders, and a couple of books."

"Which ones?"

"Dickens, Browning, and the *Winnie-the-Pooh*."

"That's strange."

"Yeah, I know."

"And?" Hunter was looking sneaky.

He answered reluctantly. "The *Who's Who* . . ." and let it trail.

What a hoot! "You mean the one with the big paragraph on you?"

Hunter scowled. All I allowed myself was a broad grin. This was getting better and better.

"Your ladycat's got a great sense of humor."

His chin sunk into his chest and his eyes glazed over. The whole episode must have been quite a defeat for old Jockey Shorts. We called him that at Yale, and the nickname stuck over the years. One night in a drunken stupor I told Abbie about it, and Hunter has never forgiven me. I'm sure he'll never forgive me for getting him to tell me about the little burglar either. But he did, and of his own volition.

When he had finished I didn't even crack a smile. I headed straight for the booze and poured him a double Scotch, Chivas Regal. I had bourbon on the rocks. After all, it couldn't make my hangover worse, and how could I let him drink alone, in a situation like that? We both went topside for some fresh air. I set to work on the deck, and Hunter stared morosely out to sea.

"It wouldn't be so bad if I had just struck out, but I struck out with a chick who was walking off with Virginia's ring on her little finger and I didn't even recognize it!"

He sighed. "Jesus Christ, I never thought I was such an asshole!"

I refrained from comment.

"Sorry, old pal. You sure were had."

"Find her for me, McQuade."

I sat up on my haunches. "You got to be kidding?" He wasn't. "I've retired, man!"

"You've been bumming around for over a week, McQuade; you've got to be bored by now. Besides, I know you invested the money from the Jag, so you can't have much ready cash. I'll pay you, and I'll pay you well, believe me."

Hunter was right; I had invested the money for safe-keeping. Maryanne and I hadn't been back to the Blue Fox all week, and Maryanne loved to eat well. I figured it would be better to stash the cash. I knew I'd have enough left to last me another three months if I rationed it out cautiously. If I kept up appearances instead, and kept up with Maryanne, I figured I had enough to last me one month, no more.

"Look, Jess. I was a good lawyer. Even first-rate. But I don't know a damned thing about detective work. That takes a special kind of talent. Besides, I'm thinking of joining the public defender's office."

A big lie. I had come to loathe law in my one week of freedom. During that time, Buz had been locked up twice for drunk and disorderly conduct and had spent three days in the clinker each time because he didn't have the bread for a lawyer, let alone bail. I had never met anyone like him that I liked before, other than some down-and-outs I had refused to defend over the years. Down-and-outs like Buz. My new life was forcing me to take some stock, but none of it was sorted out yet.

I frowned, thinking of the night I had just spent with Michelle, my new friend from next door. It had been wrong; more than wrong, and I knew it. Hunter misunderstood the frown and jumped in with, "I'll pay you two hundred and fifty dollars a day plus expenses, Mac. Try it for a couple of weeks. You can quit if you don't get anyplace. Let's say I'm staking you for your little sabbatical."

"You're nuts," I responded. "I don't look anything

like Lou Archer, although God knows I'm tougher than Archie Goodwin."

All Hunter said was, "Come on, Trav. I know you're dying to have a go at it . . ."

I tried another tack. "Be serious, Jess. I wouldn't have the slightest idea of how to track down the little lady."

"Two hundred and fifty dollars plus expenses."

"Why me, for Christ's sake?"

"Who else do I know who would keep quiet about it?"

He had a point there. I stood up and paced around over by the railing. The idea of trying to track down the broad in the blue leotard was intriguing.

Hunter was persistent. "Don't give me that 'I don't know how' bullshit, Mac. You know plenty about investigating. You did enough on the Buford case to win it in court."

"That was over a year ago, Jess. Don't try to pressure me; it won't work."

I turned and looked out over the bay. I sure as hell could use the bread and, much as I hated to admit it, I was already getting bored with the loafer's life. It appeared that once work-oriented, forever work-bound. Playing detective would give me something to do.

"Three hundred dollars a day plus expenses. Pick up the Jag again, if you want to."

"I prefer the scooter."

We looked at each other; both of us knew Hunter had me. I've always liked dark girls, especially dancers. They could really wrap their legs around you.

"I'll try it for a week, old pal, but that's it."

Hunter beat a quick retreat, calling over his shoulder, "I'll send you a check tomorrow." He knew when to quit.

Actually, Jim Diamond had done the research for me on the Buford case. I didn't know a thing about that kind of investigating. As soon as Hunter left I gave Jim a call and woke him up. He wasn't working. I suggested lunch at Poole's, figuring I'd charge it to old Jess. I got there a little early, parked the bike, and sat down at the bar with some more bourbon. The view was tremendous; there were at least four lovelies already eating at scattered tables. One, a blonde, gave me the eye, and I gave it right back.

I must have looked a little out of place—no tie; turtleneck and pressed jeans. (Ida insisted on coming down to clean the boat and ironed every piece of clothing I had shipped there as well. She can't stand to see me in rumpled clothes; hence, the ironed jeans.) Jim looked even worse; his shirt must have been a vintage 1965 and looked like he had been wearing it steadily since then to sleep in. Jim and I get along very well; he dropped out years ago and must have always sensed I had too, in my soul at least.

We ordered coq au vin (the special of the day) and chablis and then settled in for business. I told him as little as possible, not even Hunter's name, which he would have loved knowing. Jim had been trying to crash our Sunday night poker game for years; this would have given him a lever in, but Hunter's an older friend of mine and he doesn't like Jim, so I kept quiet about who had been ripped off. Jim was as intrigued by the girl as I was.

"If you strike out, man, send her my way."

"We'll both have to wait in line. First she goes to jail, remember?"

He looked sad for a moment and then thoughtful. "You might as well start at the beginning, Mac. First, I'd hit Vesuvio's, then Lord Jim's; and as a last resort, I'd try some of those spots along Union Street. They're 'in' right now with the swinging singles. Maybe you'll get a lucky break and some bartender'll recognize her description."

"She wouldn't be caught dead in a place like that!" —McQuade, the knight in shining armor defending the honor of a fair and virtuous damsel. Virtuous as hell!

"Relax, buddy. I don't think she would either, but you gotta case them out, to be sure."

"What then?"—McQuade, the pessimist.

"Look up some dance-supply stores and see if any of the clerks remember her. If she was in, someone'll remember, with a build and face sounding the way you described them."

And that was that. The rest of the meal we discussed Angela, a little lovely both of us had scored with once upon a time—she owned a boutique in Sausalito and was still a friend of mine—and the lack of work, which I was still sort of pleased about and Jim was not. He told me if I ran into any snags trying to find the burglar to give him a call.

I tried Vesuvio's that afternoon, plus a couple of places Jim hadn't mentioned, and struck out, badly. One barkeep laughed, "Hey, mister, maybe I'll quit and help you look. She sounds like a real piece." By the time I got back to *Bessie*, my head felt like it was going to sink into the bay. I wasn't so young anymore; the booze was catching up.

Buz was sitting on the ramp leading down to both our

boats, stone sober. He had seen me, so it was too late to turn back. There was an awkward silence. I sat down next to him. I had to bring up my night with Michelle; there was no other way.

"I feel like a shit, man. It won't happen again."

Buz was staring into space and didn't seem to hear. Suddenly I felt wiped out; it had been a long couple of days, too much going in, too little out.

"When I met Michelle, she was wandering around the boatyards, bummed out on her folks, some twenty-year-old creep, and cocaine. She was sixteen. That's why she's so uptight when I go on a drunk. We cleaned up her act . . ."

Shit. "You said she fucked like a bunny."

He waved the phrase away with one paw. "Just a game we play . . ."

"Some game!"

"Yeah . . . nobody wins . . . everybody's sorry."

Sorry! I didn't know where to begin.

"You were the first in a long time."

An opening. "And the last. It was lousy for all concerned." I wanted to reassure him a whole lot—and it was true—but it came out stuffy, sounded like a crock. So I added, "I was pretty far gone and she was uptight—at you, I guess. It started out as sort of comforting each other." Some comfort. "I'm sorry."

Buz stood up. "I just wanted to make sure you understood." He paused—"It may take a while for me to come around."—and was gone, loping across the gravel and bumming a ride into town.

For someone who'd had a lot of success early, I had a

lot to learn. I went below deck, took a hot shower, and sacked out. By the time I woke up, I felt even worse about the whole rotten episode. I realized I liked both Buz and Michelle—the first people I'd felt that way about in a long time, despite their idiosyncracies—and had probably ruined it all for a meaningless roll in the hay. Living on the boat for even twelve days, and seeing how other people lived, seemed to be affecting how my mind worked, if not my actions. My hide seemed to be getting too thick anyhow. Maybe if I got involved in Buz's fight to stay in the marina, it'd begin to make up for my totally shitty behavior to both of them. I sure as hell hoped so. I poured a stiff one, grabbed *The Matarese Circle*, slumped onto the Vitagenic, and dropped off early.

The next morning I was raring to go by ten thirty, a small miracle in and of itself. Maybe I just wanted to get the hell away, and finding the little dancer seemed as good an excuse as any. I tried the dance shop in Sausalito before zooming across the bay, in the hope that today would be brighter than the day before. No such luck.

In the big apple, I did even worse. By the second store, I knew it was a lost cause. The big bearded dude behind the counter laughed when I told him what I was after.

"Hey, man. You got any idea how many chicks who look like that come in here and try on leotards? Blue ones, pink ones, green ones, and even the old-fashioned black kind? Guess."

I didn't like the game. "Hundreds."

"Millions, man. Millions."

I wouldn't give up. "Dark hair, almost black, big round hazel eyes, firm little tits, no bra, good nipples, peachy skin that you'd love to get your hands on. What do you say fella? Think back."

He told me to forget it, he had other work to do. "Stop bugging me, man. Can't you take no for an answer?"

The third guy—sallow, ugly, pimply fellow with horn-rims—had much the same reaction. "Split, man, and don't come back." I would have liked to ram my fist down his bloated, blotchy throat.

"If I spot her, I don't think I'd want to tell you about it. I like that type myself."

Real wise ass. From the doorway I called back sotto voce, so all the customers would hear, "Don't worry, buster. She doesn't dig pimply flakes like you, anyhow." The toeshoe hit the door frame right above where my head had been.

Back at the boat, Buz and Michelle were painting the trim on their little sloop. Everyone nodded at everyone else, but no one said word one.

I mixed up a batch of extradries below and nursed the first one in the tub. By the time my robe was belted, I had made a decision. I would make it up to the couple next door, and I would find Hunter's dancer. The gig was far from up, although the dance-supply places had gotten me no place. There were still more bars I could hit, and if they drew a blank, I knew I could find something else. Because, I was discovering I kind of liked the work.

ANTONIA
6.

MARCH 14 WAS A BEAUTIFUL DAY. THE AIR
was crisp and clear, the sky an amazing shade of aqua,
not a cloud in sight, and there was no fog across the bay.
Spring was clearly coming, and Christopher and I re-
joiced by eating outside on the plaza. All winter we had
retreated to the cafeteria—it was unpleasant sitting outside in the dank, moist air—and both of us were relieved
to be outside again. It was like reliving those few warm
weeks when we had first met. A Frisbee game was in
uproarious progress behind us; two of the players kept
after us, and before long we had caught the spirit and
joined in. I leaped into a very tall blond to make a

stupendous catch and almost dislocated my shoulder. Christopher kissed it, though, and that made everything seem okay. After the game we both had a doughnut and some hot tea. Then he went to lecture his freshmen, and I retreated to the library's archives.

At about three in the afternoon, I made my way to the cluttered, microscopic room I call "office." There was a note on my desk: "Call Wendy." Leslie had taken the message, but she was nowhere in sight. I called the number but got no answer. I figured the group had all gone to the park, given that it was the first warmish day we had had in months, and didn't think much about it. Until I got to Wendy's and saw the note tacked to the front door.

"Tony—we are at Kaiser. Rachel fell off a swing. Don't think it's too serious. Come on over."

Not "too" serious! What the hell did that mean? How could Rachie fall off a swing? She had great balance. Probably Marius pushed her off; the damned pest was always running her over on his bicycle, or pushing her over, or, his latest trick, biting her on the stomach. Shit. I hoped she was all right.

I hitched a ride and made it to the hospital in about twenty minutes. The first thing I saw was Rachel, on top of a long metal table, her arm in an enormous white cast. I had to fight to keep back the tears; she wasn't supposed to comfort me, I was the one whose job it was to hold and kiss and love.

"Mommy! Oh, Mommy, it hurts."

And with that, she practically leaped off the table into my arms. I kissed her hair, and loved her, and made her laugh by laughing at the huge white glacier on her arm. Within minutes, she had forgotten the fall and the doctors and the injection and the x-ray and the pain. Pretty much, at any rate.

Actually, her spirits were in such good shape and she was so glad to see me that she launched into a detailed and charming description of her mishap. I could never re-create it verbatim. The gist of it was that she had been swinging quite happily and "really high, Mommy—you should've seen," when Nicole ran in front of the swing. Now you have to remember, Nicole is Rachel's very best friend in the whole world. When Nicole's mom sent her to Wendy's Place, Rach carried on so much that I had to follow suit. Whenever the two of them see each other (which is five days a week, at least) they run into arms and legs, and hug and kiss and tell each other everything that has happened since last they met. So. If Rachel had swung forward she would have hit Nicole and given her quite a thump. Instead of doing that to her very best friend in the whole world, my kid threw herself off the swing backward and missed the sand. She smashed into the wall and was unconscious for a couple of minutes. I'm glad I missed that part; even thinking about it gives me the creeps.

Nicole and her mother were at the hospital, too, so Nicole filled in the details that Rachel didn't know or couldn't remember; the account was quite vivid.

Everybody was there except Wendy. Apparently she was off haggling with the doctor about the bill. Since she's a member of the Kaiser plan—she can afford the monthly insurance payments; I cannot—I figured she was trying to take responsibility for the bill, which could have made it very small. I went looking for Wendy, hoping to help with the arguing. I've gotten very good at that sort of thing.

I found her huddled over a desk in a little alcove around the corner from Rachel's stall with a rotund little man in white. Wendy had her Kaiser card in her hand and was talking to the round, balding type very earnestly. She seemed to be getting nowhere. He turned to me.

"Can I help you?"

"I'm Rachel's mother. Sorry I'm so late, Wendy, but I never got the message."

"I'm afraid you're going to have a pretty stiff bill here"—Baldy looked very severe—"the hospital demands payment within a week."

"But Rachel wasn't at home when she broke her arm, she was at Wendy's Place. It's a licensed day-care center, covered by very adequate insurance."

"We've been all through that, Mrs. Weiner. The center does have some coverage, but it's only for accidents that occur on the premises. The only full coverage is for the card holder, Miss Graham. Look at the small print here, on the back of the rate card."

We all bent over the desk. There it was, plain as day.

The bald-headed schmuck added, "So you would have to pay the bill in any event." He was looking directly at me, there was no denying it.

"So what would you say if I told you I don't have it?"

He looked pained. "I'm afraid a collection agency would take over, and they'd give you plenty of heartache."

"Well, at least you're not going to take the cast off and break her arm again."

No one laughed. The doctor coughed and suggested Wendy check with her insurance man. "You should get yourself covered for this sort of thing." Wendy stood her ground and glared at him.

"Let me see the bill." I broke the silence.

I had expected it to be bad but not that bad. Not only had they x-rayed the kid's arm, they had done a job on her head as well, because of the minor concussion. The bill was $187.37. I stuffed the bill in my purse and turned on my heel.

"It's comforting to know that Kaiser isn't a typical bureaucracy and that its employees bend the rules to suit the needy!"

The doctor was speechless and, I might add, quite uncomfortable. He should have been: the cost was outrageous. Where the hell did average people get the bread for this kind of emergency? What did they do when the collection agency came knocking at their door? Rip off a liquor store and end up in county jail? Clean houses in the hills six days a week?

Wendy followed me around the corner and laid her hand on my shoulder. "Tony, I won't let you pay that whole bill. We should at least split it!"

"No, you've got enough money problems. I'd rather you kept your doors open than pay for my kid's broken arm."

"But she broke it because I wasn't watching."

"No, she didn't. There was nothing you could have done, even if you had been watching."

"Well, I certainly should have been more careful

about that insurance. Goddamn it! I've been running that center for four years and paying an arm and a leg for insurance all that time. I've just assumed I was completely covered. Wait till I get ahold of that prick of an insurance agent. He told me I had the best, most comprehensive coverage there was. I wonder if I could sue the company?"

"Maybe. Why don't you ask Tim?" He was a law professor and father to Marius.

Wendy was close to tears, and she rarely cries. "Oh, Tony. I'm so damned sorry. How in the hell are you going to pay for this?"

"I don't know. Call my parents, I guess." But I was lying. I knew where the money would come from; I just couldn't tell Wendy.

Although, damn it, I wasn't pleased about it! I hadn't pulled a job since I ran into Hunter III in his elevator. What I hauled away from his place netted me over seven hundred dollars (I kept the ring) and had lasted a couple of months, once I paid Wendy off. The dance lessons were going really well; I now had ten regular students, and Rachel and I were doing okay on a day-to-day basis. I had hoped that the other thing was past and done for, although I suppose I knew something like this was bound to happen, sooner or later. I guess I had just been biding my time.

That night I resurrected my "hit" list, which I had filed away under "miscellaneous," and the next afternoon made a few discreet inquiries, checking up on the boring business exec and the architect. Both were likely prospects because they were both single, with no kids or wife or steady mistress for me to worry about. The businessman lived in a triplex, with no obvious access except a back courtyard. It was possible, if he ever stayed out late enough and did it on a regular basis, but it didn't seem like a great idea. I didn't know very much about him and it would have taken too long to do the research. I already knew that the architect was punctual and could be counted on for consistency. His visiting sister was long gone since I last looked in on him; his maid came only during the day, Monday, Wednesday, and Friday, and left by three thirty.

I got right down to business by making one phone call, offering a free sample of some new nonallergenic blush-on makeup to his maid. It was a great way to confirm her schedule: she asked me to bring the sample back on a Wednesday or Friday, because those were the only days she would be there. Tuesdays and Thursdays she worked over on Knob Hill.

Wednesday morning I cut two classes and hastened over to my architect's Victorian mansion. I took the bus across the bridge and a cable car to his corner. I brought several different shades of makeup with me, so I could get a chance to really look around while the maid, whose name was Mary, examined her loot. She was a nice lady and offered me some hot tea—it was one of those windy, nasty, foggy San Francisco days, and I had forgotten my jacket because Berkeley wasn't so cold. I stood on the stoop shivering but trying not to.

The kitchen was done in bright, primary colors and was smashing. His dishes were from Jensen; so was the silverware. He had three unmatched, antique candleholders perched on top of the cabinet next to the sink and a beautiful copper kettle on the stove. Both seemed easily hockable. The copper pot was one of thousands; the candle gizmos could each be taken to separate dealers. The tea was delicious; she served it with honey.

Living room, dining room, den, and kitchen were on the main level, two bedrooms with separate baths filled out the second floor; he had his office up top.

"Mr. Beckworth says he gets ideas on the weekends, so he's specially concerned that I clean out the office real well. He says he can't work when it's messy. I've been here two years, come this June."

She was definitely a nice lady; I was pretty sure Beckworth would know she hadn't ripped him off. I made a mental note to be a little sloppy so he'd know for sure it hadn't been her. If he had talked with her even an eighth as much as I had, he would know she couldn't leave a mess behind her. Even her uniform was starched.

So. He was a good target, with lots of little memorabilia lying around the living room as well as perched atop his kitchen cabinets—silver Mexican ashtrays, worth many pennies; handsome, tiny pieces of sculpture in the master bedroom; and a couple of gold cups for cigarettes. He seemed to prefer Marlboros. Everything was compact and easy to carry, perfect for me.

Of course, I hadn't cased out his personal life yet, so I didn't know his schedule precisely. But even if he spent one regular evening out a week, or one hour a week after seven, so it'd be dark, I'd be okay. The house next door had a back porch that leaned out over Beckworth's roof. I knew I could throw a line from the porch to the roof and loop onto the railing with a grappling hook. The rope would have to be pulled very taut and would slope down quite a bit—there was about a one-and-a-half-floor difference between the porch and the roof. But I had my pulley wheel: I would just have to learn to use it.

The building with the porch had seven apartments —one on the first floor and two on all the other floors—and the porch was a lean-to built off of the roof. Apparently, it was used by all the tenants. The front door wasn't locked. I could walk right on up to the top; if anyone heard me up here, they would just assume I was a tenant or a friend of a tenant. No hassle. Actually, the setup was beginning to look ideal.

The following morning I called Professor Warren and told him I still felt lousy—I thought I must have the flu—and would probably be out the week. I suggested that if he needed me to do anything special, Leslie could drop it by the apartment on her way home. He told me not to worry and got very solicitous over the phone.

"You're the best student I've had in over five years, Antonia, even with your little writing problem, and I wouldn't want to lose you to the flu. Stay in bed a few extra days if you need to; we'll hold the fort over here. Would you like Louise and me to watch Rachel for you?"

For some reason, his question annoyed me. I found myself wanting to ask him if Louise wanted to watch

Rachel five days a week, so I could make it through graduate school on the pittance they called a fellowship, without experiencing so much agony. Warren was a plodder, but I was the one with a problem! Although he probably voted every year to raise fellowships in keeping with rising inflation, he never gave a thought to the fact that the amount he voted for was infinitely lower than what any normal person—let alone a couple or family—needed to live on. Or the fact that we were kept so busy with our own studies, plus our "advisor's" 'shit work', as my officemates called it, that it was virtually impossible to hold a job for the hours necessary to make working a worthwhile endeavor. The angry rush of words racing through my head came as such a shock that I just stifled them, managing nevertheless to graciously decline his offer.

Rachel was a little lamb that morning. She kept quiet the whole time I was talking to Warren, although she stared at me with her eyes wide open and her little mouth clamped shut. I talked to him with a handkerchief over the phone and pitched my voice low, so I'd sound awful. When I hung up, we both looked at each other and Rachel said, "Are you all right, Mommy?" I picked her up and put her under the covers with me and we played hide and seek for ten minutes.

She looked so worried; as angry as I felt, it was still pretty obvious to my bright little kid that I was quite miserable about the deceit. Unhappily, I told her it was sometimes impossible not to lie, but I still felt awful about doing it. By the time breakfast was over she seemed to have forgotten all about it.

"I'm gonna get everyone to sign my arm, except

Timmy, because he can't write his name yet," she informed me on the bus ride over to Wendy's.

"Why don't you let him draw a picture on it, Rach? He'll be hurt if he's the only one who can't sign it; don't you think?"

Rachel sat back and thought about it, and then her face relaxed into a comfortable grin.

"You're right, Mommy. He likes to color. I think he'd like that."

She took my hand and gave it a squeeze. She didn't let go until we were inside school. All the kids crowded around to look at the cast, and Rachie dropped my hand so she could more easily command center stage. I left, unnoticed.

The bus ride across the bridge was a quick one, because there were very few passengers—it was a bit past rush hour and a little too early for shoppers. My first stop was Fransly and Croft, the big firm Beckworth worked for. It had its office in the Cannery. I had a cup of tea in a coffee shop with a view of the main entrance and waited for lunch. He came out at 12:15 with two other guys, both sort of square, and they headed for the BV, a small bar near the Cannery famous for its Irish coffee and chili. I followed behind and decided to go inside and eat too. If I could sit near them, I might learn something worth knowing. What a waste of $2.75! They talked shop for an hour and a half and only broke off once to discuss how badly Robert Parish had played the night before. If I didn't happen to like basketball, I wouldn't have had any idea what they were talking about.

When they went back to the office, I hopped a bus

over to Russian Hill and tried to get a little more familiar with the neighborhood. There were no really big buildings around: apparently Beckworth merely designed them, choosing to live nowhere in their vicinity. Most of the houses on his street and the two blocks on either side of it were little town houses, at the most two families to a dwelling, although two or three had been turned into plush little apartment houses, like the one next door to Beckworth's own place. Ladies strolled around with babies in carriages, women in stylish suits came and went, and several maids carried garbage to and from the curb, walked poodles, and finally locked up and went back to the Fillmore District to look after their own families. All in all, it was a quiet neighborhood. At four thirty I made my way back to Fransly and Croft to see where Beckworth would go when he got off work. He walked home. My legs were getting tired, but I followed him anyway. At six I had to get back to Berkeley to pick up Rachie. I wanted to stay and see where he went, but I hadn't been able to find a suitable sitter for the evening. Someone who didn't know I was supposed to be sick, and someone who Rachel liked. Friday night she was having a sleep-over date with Nicole, so I would be able to do a thorough case-out then.

Saturday I had a very lucky break. Beckworth met a chubby but pretty secretary type in the middle of the afternoon and they went to Blum's for ice cream. I had a cone a few tables away from them. The girl talked in a rather loud voice. I could have run over and kissed her when she blurted out, "Oh, I love ACT. And *Cyrano de Bergerac*'s supposed to be the best show they've done all

season. Wednesday night would be perfect, Rickie!"
With that she leaned over the table and gave him a
loud smack on the lips. He didn't seem to mind, keeping
his arm around her and whispering hoarsely that he'd
pick her up for dinner at 6:45. He wanted to go home
and freshen up after work, as he assumed she would.
That was all I needed. I caught the next bus back,
picked up Rachel at Nicole's, and took her to the park.
She was a little bit afraid to go on the swing at first, but I
stood in back of her, and soon she was swinging happily
away. She held on awfully well for a one-handed girl.

We had ice cream and cookies for dessert, and then I
gave Christopher a call. I hadn't been able to see him for
almost a week, and he was pretty pissed. I had told him I
was sick, also, and cautioned Rachel not to say
anything—"We had a little fight, monkeykins, so I
didn't want to see him." She nodded, my partner for
life. I hated lying to her, but how could I explain what
was really up?

Christopher came over at eight. He said he wanted to
see Rachel, and she went to bed by eight thirty. He
asked her if she was all right, and she just shrugged her
little shoulders.

"Yeah, I guess. You gonna help me with the puzzle
before I go to bed, Christopher?"

He had brought her another dilly. They played for
over forty-five minutes, or he played and she watched,
and then we put her to bed. She hugged and kissed us
and got two stories, and then we were alone.

"You seeing anyone else, Tony?"

"No. I told you I wasn't over the phone. I felt lousy all

week and I hate seeing anyone when I feel that way. If Rachel didn't live here, I wouldn't have seen her either."

After I said it, it felt true to me. Because when I am sick, I do hate to see people. Michael never understood that; it was one of the issues he insisted broke up our marriage. Once when we were fighting I told him that I found it a lot more serious that I didn't want to see him when I was healthy. He stormed out and didn't come back till morning. It wasn't a nice thing for me to have said. That night, Christopher wouldn't let it lie, and I felt like I was being pulled apart. I couldn't be honest, but I still felt guilty that I was lying about what I was up to.

"I know you won't believe this, Christopher." I rubbed my eyes for sympathy. "I've gotten behind at school; I have two sets of papers to grade and exams are coming up in two weeks. I'm going to be busy next week, too."

There was a very ominous silence.

"All of next week?"

"Oh, I don't know. Maybe only till Thursday. I should be caught up by Thursday. Or enough caught up so the distraction of working together won't be too great."

Christopher sat there staring at me. I loved him then; he looked so downtrodden. I kneeled at his feet and put my head in his lap.

"Oh, Christopher. I hate not seeing you. I feel lonely and out of sorts and afraid."

"What are you afraid of?"

Jesus, how had that come out. "I'm afraid you'll walk out and never come back. Rachie sure would miss you . . ."

He began to stroke my head. "Tony, Tony, Tony. Why do you make it all so difficult. Instead of fighting off the monsters alone, you could call out 'help' once in a while. I'm here, Tony. I'm not leaving."

I looked into his deep dark eyes, and we kissed a long, lingering kiss. But I couldn't help feeling uneasy, because I didn't think he could accept the truth. He hadn't offered me a dime in weeks, and he hadn't asked me how Rachel and I were doing, or what we were doing, for that matter. It wasn't an oversight. He didn't want to know. Which didn't bode too well for our future.

Even so, the sex was okay that night. Hell, it was lovely. Christopher was a sensitive and adventurous lover, and it was always good, always. Maybe that's why I felt so sad after he left that morning and why I remember it now. It was lovely, but it wasn't the same. Something in me died that night; I knew Christopher and I could only go so far together, and it made me feel an aching void. Maybe the way I was becoming, no one would ever want me for keeps. I was a robber, a burglar, a cat thief. When I was broke, I climbed into other people's homes and ripped them off. I rationalized by telling myself I only robbed bad guys, but was that really the point? I still robbed people.

This time, when Rachie broke her arm, I didn't even agonize over what to do. I knew. Right away. But even worse than that, I felt a little excited about the whole thing. Just like I used to when as an undergraduate I was going to write a new paper on a subject no one had dared tackle before. I was going to rob someone, but I was going to do it so well no one would ever know.

When I wrote a paper at Antioch, I never did it the same way twice. The style and tone were always different. It was more of a challenge that way. Since I could no longer work that way for Warren, I was fulfilling the need to be creative with my little rip-offs. I purposely chose the architect, not because of the sister or his schedule or anything rational, but because he lived in a town house, and robbing it would be totally different from robbing Hunter. I couldn't possibly get to the roof and swing down. I would have to find another way. Then there was the added excitement of the other building, the unknown quantity of its tenants and all their friends. Finally, there was the rope and the pulley wheel. In the beginning I had sworn never to try it—too iffy, too dangerous. But now, well, now it excited me. I must have been a little nuts.

After dropping Rachel off the next morning, I came back to the apartment to deposit some groceries I had picked up for dinner. The doorbell rang about three minutes after I got home. I peered out the window and almost died. Professor Warren was standing there with a brown bag full of groceries, humming. I ripped off my clothes and dived into my nightgown, hitting the buzzer as I pulled it over my head. I pulled out the couch, unmade the bed, and rumpled the covers in ten seconds flat.

I left the groceries out and slouched over to answer the door, grabbing a Kleenex on the way.

"Professor Warren! I don't think you should come in, I might contaminate you."

"Don't worry about that, Antonia. I never catch any of

the children's colds. Here. I thought you and Rachel might need some groceries. Where is the little lamb?"

"Wendy came and picked her up. Today must be my lucky day. She brought us some supplies, too. I was just unpacking them."

He smiled. "I hope we didn't double up."

"Oh, that's all right. If you did, it'll be doubly appreciated." I smiled, telling myself, "Be gracious, Tony. You'll still get to San Francisco on time to watch Beckworth eat lunch."

"You're welcome, my dear." Old chubs chuckled. "Even illness hasn't dulled your wit."

He was a nice man; just very limited. He could no more think of the overall size of graduate fellowships, or the horrendous cost of mass education and how they went hand in hand, than accept a paper written about a familiar subject in an unfamiliar way. Both possibilities were too damned dangerous.

The phrase "beware of the 'nice' people" flitted through my head as I took the groceries and started to unpack them; but the prof insisted I go to bed while he did it. He brought me a cup of tea with honey in it and a slice of lemon, straightened out the covers I had rumpled up so carefully, and told me he had graded the papers—I didn't have to worry about it. I thanked him, with a great ring of truth. If he hadn't, I don't know if I could have done them before seeing Christopher on Thursday. Professor Warren saw himself out and left me to sleep away the morning in peace. Or so he thought.

By 10:45 I was on the bus, looking out at the bay and

drinking in the panorama before me. No matter how long I live here, I will never get used to the view. It is breathtaking, especially on one of those crisp, winter days, and it was one of those days.

I felt thankful that Professor Warren had graded those papers so I could enjoy it, and was suddenly overwhelmed by guilt pangs. Could I really blame my situation on Warren's inability to use his brains, along with all the other plodders, or was I just becoming callous myself? My life really had turned very topsy-turvy.

As I rounded the corner of Beach and Hyde, I almost bumped into Beckworth. He had left his office ten minutes early and was on his way to lunch with the same boring companions. I decided to skip eating when they went into the BV. First, I couldn't afford it. Second, I couldn't handle another boring hour and a half. Besides, I had more important things to do.

I caught a bus to the army/navy store. The same salesman was behind the desk.

"Hi ya, honey. Is the boyfriend proud o'ya? Did he ask ya where you learned your stuff?" With that he let out a loud guffaw. God, what a cretin. My stomach lurched a bit, but I dazzled the creep with a special smile.

"Yeah." I grinned up at him. "I did so well, he wants to take me mountain hopping."

"Fantastic! You'll love it. It's real exciting. When I was a ranger, back in '52"—here we go again, I thought—"me and this other fella would go out sometimes at night, when the boss was asleep, and do some hopping.

Real excitin' stuff. Nothing to it, once you get the hang of it."

"That's what I'm worried about," I cut in. "Getting the hang of it. I'm not worried about impressing Joey anymore. I think I impressed him a little too much. Now I'm just scared to death. What if I miss and land in between two peaks?" A tear fell. Beckworth's roof was only four flights up, but I really was scared stiff about it.

His whole face lit up. "You want another little lesson?"

I shook my head vigorously. "Is there anyplace we could do it that would be sort of real, so I could actually practice?"

He bit. "I could take you up to the Sierras tomorrow. It's my day off. In an hour you'd be going real well."

I looked at him wide-eyed, nauseating myself and anyone else within seeing and hearing distance. "Oh, that would be wonderful."

Take five seconds. "I can trust you, can't I?"

His face expressed the proper amount of horror.

"Little lady, I think of you as my own daughter. Ask Jack here. He'll tell you what I'm like."

Jack assured me Ted was open and aboveboard. He had taken several customers up to the Sierras, both male and female, and they all continued to patronize the store. What better proof could I want? None, I answered, and decided to take the chance. I told Ted I'd meet him in front of the store by eight thirty.

Roaring away in his car the following morning, I tried not to feel anxious. I shouldn't have worried about it. He spent four hours telling me about his life as a ranger and was still talking when we started to climb. He had taken along enough rope for two, some hooks, and two pulley wheels. He was amazed to discover I could carry my share of rope.

"You're a tough cookie for such a tiny little thing." He squinted in my direction.

We had driven as far up the smallest mountain as we could and had gotten out to climb the rest of the way on foot. We wound our way around and got to the top in half an hour. The air was light up so high and I found myself breathing quicker than I had been in the car. The second peak was about fifteen feet away, on a downward slope. The angle was similar to the one from Beckworth's roof. I looked down and almost passed out. The drop was a good deal more than four stories. Maybe I should have taken him to Beckworth's building and given him some hush money, I thought to myself. It would have been safer.

We practiced throwing the rope, until I could get the hook to hit and hold five times running. Then Ted said I was ready to go. I didn't feel it, but Ted gave me a little push and away I went. I landed very smoothly and even managed to look graceful coming down. Ted yahooed and hoorayed on the other peak, jumped up and down, fingers stuck in his mouth for the appropriate whistle, and generally made an ass of himself. He swung over without a second thought, while I prepared to go back the other way. It was a little harder going uphill but not much. I figured it would be a good thing to learn, just in case I had to make a quick escape back to Beckworth's neighbors' porch. Ted was right; within half an hour I felt like a pro. We sailed back down the mountain, Ted rambling on about the good old ranger days and nudging and bumping me as much as he could, and me thinking about the booty I was going to haul away in a couple of days. I felt positively euphoric; this was going to be fun. Ted swore he wanted to drive all the way back on the return trip, and I fell asleep on the back seat, numbed by the sound of his voice recounting past adventures. He had had millions of them, apparently.

I told Ted I was going to Ghirardelli Square, a good central (and anonymous) location, and he dropped me off at around seven. I bought a pint of chocolate ice cream for Rach, looked around for a few minutes, and decided to head back to Berkeley.

By Wednesday I was itching to go. Mrs. Guerin came over to sit for Rachel and by six had prepared a sumptuous feast for her.

"Why don't you stay and have something yourself, Tony? You're wasting away to nothing in those little dungarees of yours."

I assured her I liked being thin and that I would eat in San Francisco before I went to the dance concert, and then I split. I had left the suitcase in the downstairs hall, so Mrs. G. wouldn't ask me about it. It was quite a schlepp getting it to the bus stop, but I made it without mishap in about ten minutes, stopping and starting several times along the way. I don't think anyone saw me. The bus took half an hour going across the bridge; I was on Beckworth's corner by 7:05. His lights were all out. I felt utterly content and not the least bit scared. Excited, yes, but not scared. "You've come a long way, baby," I sang to myself as I hauled the suitcase up the stoop of the adjoining building.

I hadn't much thought about the problems of getting

the thing up five flights of carpeted stairs, and I should have. It took forty-five minutes of sheer panic, waiting for someone to come out of an apartment and into my path, wonder who I was, and blab about it to someone the next day. I tried to be very quiet as I lifted, heaved, lugged, and tugged, and only dropped the damned thing once. By the time I reached the fifth and last floor, I was lightheaded. I bopped out to the porch and was there before I could stop myself.

A petite and stylish blonde was watering her plants in the right-hand corner. She turned, saw me, and smiled. I couldn't very well hide the suitcase and had no idea what to do. She looked me up and down and decided to say hello.

Forcing myself to smile, I let out a "Hi!"

She looked at me, waiting. Luckily I blushed. "I didn't want to leave it in the hall. You know . . ." I let the end of my sentence trail off suggestively and looked at the ground, praying there was a well-known lech in the building that she would assume I was coming to visit. She just stared at me, looking quite hostile. Then I saw the click behind her face as she fit me into the right groove, saying, "Be careful, honey. Tom's notorious around these parts."

I looked down embarrassed and whispered, "I know that. I can't help it."

"Well . . ." She went back to her plants, dispensed with them, told me she had to run, and added before she left, "He gets home by eight. I'd invite you in, but I've got company myself tonight."

By then I was freezing. The sweat had poured

through my blue leotard, lining the inside of the white heavy-knit cardigan Mrs. Guerin had insisted I wear. "You'll catch your death of cold, child, and we can't have that, can we?" I peeled off the sweater, but that only made it worse. I was shivering and my teeth were knocking into each other, so I put it back on and went to work. The quicker I could get over to the adjoining roof, the better. I unpacked the rope and ran the suitcase downstairs, stashing it just inside the door to the basement. I swung the rope around my head and flung it across to Beckworth's roof. It caught on the first throw. I worked fast, pulling the rope taut, tying it securely onto the porch with the kind of knot that unties with the proper pressure from the other end, attached the wheel, and started across.

It was much harder breaking properly between two buildings than between mountain peaks, and I stopped dead center, terrified for my life. I really wasn't sure I could break hard enough to miss the side of Beckworth's building. I swung there for what felt like hours, trying to catch my breath and calm my stomach, and slowly started out again, trying not to put any speed into my movements whatsoever. Going back would have been just as hard as moving ahead, so what else could I have done? Inching along, I felt my teeth clench and my hair prickle; I was sure I heard someone up on that porch. There was nothing on the roof for anyone to see except the end of the rope I was hanging from, knotted to a small bar that ran the length of one side of the porch, and it was unlikely anyone could notice that in the dark. If they looked over the edge, down into the alley, I was a goner. I forced myself to look straight ahead and keep moving. A knot ran up my spine and stopped at the nape of my neck. It would take hours to loosen up. I managed to come to a stop a hair's-breadth from the side of the building, held the wheel with one hand, and grasped the ledge of the roof with the other. I pulled myself up and over without any difficulty and stood there, shaking like a leaf. I couldn't believe I had been excited an hour before. What an asshole, I thought to myself. This is no fun at all.

Then I got super careless, jerking open the door leading from the roof down a narrow stairway to Beckworth's study. A light was on. I stood on the landing, holding the door ajar, and listened. Nothing. I carefully and quietly closed the door and stood there some more. Still nothing. He could have been working at his desk, drawing a floor plan, but that would have made a noise of some kind, I reasoned to myself as I inched down the stairs. I didn't know whether to bypass the office entirely or look in to ease my mind. I looked in.

Nothing. He had just left a light on. I leaned against the doorjamb, feeling very faint, and closed my eyes in an attempt to pull myself together. I had not thought this one out clearly enough. Bumping into the girl on the roof was a ridiculous mistake. Now someone had seen me. Mistake two: I hadn't checked out Beckworth's place carefully enough; I should have seen that light from the street. I felt angry and frightened and a bit like crying, but I stifled it and got moving. Best to get in fast, lift the stuff, and scram.

A half hour later I was on my way out the door with

my stash—two copper pots, the antique candleholders, three Mexican ashtrays, one gold cigarette cup, three hundred-dollar bills that were stuffed inside it (rich men all seemed to leave ready cash lying around)—when I remembered Mary, the maid. I ran back to the living room and sprinkled ashes all over the rug, threw a couple of books around, and hurled some couch cushions to the floor. Then I got out fast.

I hid the suitcase in the downstairs hall and was in my door by nine thirty. Mrs. G. wouldn't take more than $3.50, so I quit haggling over fifty cents, thanked her, and sank into my easy chair. I downed the sandwich she had left me in two minutes, pulled out the couch, and turned the light out. For the first time ever, I didn't look in on Rachie before nodding off—I didn't want to chance her waking up and seeing me; I was much too shaky.

McQUADE
7.

THE NIGHT OF APRIL 9 WAS A BITCH: IT STANDS
out in my mind, although I've spent a lot of hours trying
to forget it. Maryanne walked out on me in the middle
of dinner at the Blue Fox. We hadn't been there in
months, so I had decided to live it up big and had put on
a suit (navy pinstripe with yellow shirt, flowered tie—
super chic) and picked her up in a cab. I ordered the
best champagne, to go with the roast beef and Yorkshire
pudding, and had planned to finish up the evening with
a stroll by the bay in Marina Park followed by a quick
cab for two back to the boat. A first for me and
Maryanne: she had never spent the night on *Bessie*. Un-

fortunately, she didn't see the occasion the same way I did. She wanted a ring and a firm commitment (day of the week, no less!), and nothing short of that seemed to do it for her. When she realized I had planned the whole ritzy evening with nothing more than a sleep-over date in mind, she freaked. Stood up and got out. I sat there holding the bottle of champagne in the middle of a toast to our first night in my home together. Christ!

The cab ride back to Sausalito was lonely as hell; the driver dropped me in front of slip 23 and I went aboard. Alone. I took out the carrot juice and poured myself a double dose.

About a month ago, Michelle convinced me that booze slows down the thinking process. We were both working on Buz. We had all been on a nodding acquaintance through Christmas, and then my boat sprung a leak. Buz saw me hopping around the deck being totally ineffective—I sailed boats but didn't fix them. He came aboard. Within one hour, no more leak and very little enmity. That's Buz. Now we are all pretty tight. If Michelle and I can get him to ignore his old lady— mother, that is—we should be able to quash the drinking. Michelle threw my last bottle of Crown Royal, and Buz's, overboard three days ago. He bought another, in good humor. I turned to juice. Now when I'm down, I throw some cold carrots in the blender, drink up, steep in a hot tub, and am generally revived in about an hour. That night was no exception.

By the time I hit the sack, I wasn't feeling too bad. Maryanne would cool off and come around. Michelle was sure of it, and so was I. She always had before, and if she thought it through like the smart wench she was, Maryanne'd realize she had gotten me farther down the line than I'd ever led her to believe she could. I switched on channel 5.

Good old square-jawed Van Amberg was talking straight out at the camera.

"Mr. Beckworth didn't discover the robbery until the early hours of the morning. He explained that when he returned to his home at about 1:00 A.M., he went straight to his bedroom on the second floor and didn't notice the mess the burglar had left behind in the living room. Several small antiques, as well as some small objets d'art of inestimable value, were stolen. James O'Leary, police lieutenant, had this to say about the whole affair—"

"We thoroughly questioned the neighbors in the immediate vicinity. An unknown dark-haired Caucasian female was seen on the roof of the adjoining building the evening before but was apparently visiting a young man in the same building. The burglar entered Mr. Beckworth's building from the roof, probably swinging from another building. It is unlikely a woman of small stature could have committed such a daring crime."

I found myself toasting the television screen. "Bravo, little lady! They'll never get you." Then I sat bolt upright. Jesus Christ, it probably was the same girl. I had taken a short sabbatical from finding her because I couldn't come up with a way to do it and had actually almost forgotten about her existence altogether. What with Maryanne, and getting to know the fifty-odd occupants of the marina—other than my immediate neighbors—and assessing their feelings on being kicked off their boats, I had been pretty busy. Filing papers and doing a legal tap dance. The fancying-up plans for the marina had ground to a temporary halt. We all still had a place to live. I was rebuilding my boat, with Buz's help, and getting off on my own dexterity. Hunter and I had agreed to put a halt on my weekly salary and had both studiously avoided mentioning the incident that had brought about my receiving it in the first place. Maybe it had never happened.

Van Amberg went on to describe Beckworth, applauding him for the great things he had already done for the fair city of San Francisco—actually, he had designed Hunter's building. I thought of calling CBS to suggest the fat prick deserved to be robbed for putting up that kind of crap, but thought better of it.

I got up and poured myself some more carrot juice. I thought to myself, "Could it be the same girl?"

Hunter's little thief had taken two stunning little antiques, the jewelry, and several small and terribly expensive art objects. She, too, had been dark. I knew the girl on the roof was no innocent loiterer, and was willing to bet she was Hunter's elevator chum. I made my way to the galley and took out a cold Danish.

"Why the hell did she rip Hunter off first? He isn't such a bad guy. He's a prick to women, but so are thousands of other young studs. Maybe it was his bank." I stood there wolfing down the cake; suddenly I was starved. The phone rang.

"H'lo. Mac here . . . Hi Jess, what's up?"

I dragged the phone over to the big chair and eased into it. Hunter could be a big talker.

"Yeah, I saw it and had the same idea myself. But I thought you had given up on it, man. We'll never get her, any more than the cops will."

The juice tasted good going down, but I was getting lightheaded. I hadn't had any dinner; I picked up the phone again and headed for the ice box. It was empty. I had been too lazy to go to the market in over a week, so cold cake would have to suffice.

"I'm curious too, Jess. If it is the same girl, she's not just a looker with great tits. I wouldn't mind sitting down with her and finding out what makes her tick either. What? Shit, man, I know you saw her first. Relax. Maybe I'll poke around a little bit tomorrow and see what I can come up with. Don't send a check yet, asshole. If I come up with something, we'll talk about it. How's that?"

I had to fix a leak in the foredeck in the morning and do the marketing, so I didn't hit San Francisco until way after eleven. What with juicing up the Honda and stopping for eggs with all the trimmings at Vesuvio's, as well, I didn't actually round the corner of Lurmont Terrace much before twelve. I cruised around for a few minutes to get the feel of the neighborhood—nice, real nice—parked the bike, and hiked up the hill. I approached the door of number 311, the scene of the crime, at about 12:15. A tall, skinny black woman with a babushka tied around her head came down the stairs lugging a huge garbage pail behind her, bump-bump-bump, down the stairs. I speeded it up so I'd get to her before she was back inside.

"Hi. You work in there?"

"I got nothing to say to you, mister. I haven't even

cleaned out the kitchen sink, yet. You newsmen don't know when to quit. I got nothing to say."

"Hey, wait a minute. I'm not a newsman . . ."

"No, so what are you? A cop?"

"Nope. Just a curious lawyer."

"Sorry, I got work to do, fella." She was back up the stairs.

"You want to tell me about the girl?"

That stopped her.

"What girl?"

With that she turned and looked down the stoop at me. Her hand was on the doorknob, and she was all ready to go inside and get to that kitchen sink, but for some reason my question did stop her. I felt myself getting excited: maybe I was on to something.

"The dark-haired girl from the roof."

"She wasn't up on the roof . . ."

The woman was standing up against the front door, holding herself around the chest, shivering. She let the sentence trail off and stared at me.

"It's cold out here. That girl didn't have nothing to do with this."

"Why don't you tell me about her anyway?"

"What's your name?"

"Robert McQuade. My friends call me Mac."

It took her about five seconds to make the decision.

"We'll both catch pneumonia out here. Why don't you come inside for some hot tea, Mac. My name's Mary." With that she turned, opened the door, and beckoned me in.

We sat down in the kitchen and waited for the water

to boil. The architect had great taste. The room was a bubble of color—red cabinets, flashy blue table, yellow tile—my eyes couldn't find any place to settle down. I liked it a lot.

"What roof was your girl on?"

I pointed next door. "Over there. She was seen on the porch next door the night of the robbery."

"Who saw her?"

"A blonde girl named Alison."

"I wouldn't trust her much. She never so much as gives me a how-de-do."

"You may be right. I haven't met her. I just read about it in the *Chronicle* this morning. She said a dark-haired, slender girl was up on the porch at around 7:00 P.M. and that she was carrying a heavy brown suitcase."

Mary looked perturbed when she got up to make the tea, but I knew I had to leave her alone or she wouldn't say anything at all. She turned to ask me if I wanted honey, and I said that sounded like a good idea: I'd never tried it before.

"I don't think it's the same girl."

I kept quiet.

"She came about a week and a half ago and sat right where you're sitting now, and she had honey, too. Real nice little thing; pleasant as could be. She was giving away . . . uh . . . you know, Avon samples; only it wasn't Avon, it was some other kind."

She took out a lipstick to show me. It was a brand you can only get in health-food stores. I knew because Michelle wears it too.

"She admired Mr. Beckworth's taste, especially that

little piece of sculpture sitting over there on that coffee table, and the burglar didn't take that, did he?"

She sounded almost defiant. I didn't mention the fact that the little piece of sculpture must have weighed over a hundred pounds. No thief in her right mind would have touched it.

"It could have been a different girl, Mary. No one's saying it wasn't. What was the cosmetics girl wearing? Do you remember?"

"Sure I do. She had on a tweed skirt and green sweater. She was standing there shivering away when I opened the door and pretending not to. She said it didn't seem cold when she left her house in the morning. She wore her hair tied up in back, but I could tell it was long and thick and black. She had real big eyes; they took up her whole face. Pretty, she was real pretty."

I was afraid I wouldn't be able to contain the excitement I was feeling—the outfit was wrong, but the rest fit perfectly—so I stood up.

"Nope. Doesn't sound like the right girl."

"I knew it, Mr. Mac. I knew it. She was real nice, not like those little niggers who'll take anything they can get their hands on. I keep my money right here where no one's gonna get it." She tapped her bosom.

"Whatcha lookin' at me like that for? That's what they are. Dirty little niggers. Bring the race down, that's all they do."

I had never heard anyone talk like that who wasn't white, and I didn't know quite how to respond. It came out sounding middle-class goody-goody.

"Well, I don't know, Mary. They have a pretty rough time."

"So do I and so do you, but you ain't never caught us stealing, have you? There's other things to be done."

For the first time in my life I wasn't sure of that. Conditions were tight, and not everyone's cut out to be a maid. "That's true," I argued with myself. "But there are still plenty of things she could be doing other than robbing people. Crime is wrong, no matter how you cut it." I thanked Mary for the tea and went next door on the off chance the blonde would be home. The tenth was my lucky day.

Alison McCall would have been a real knockout if her incisors faced in instead of out. As it was, they looked like little fangs and, I discovered, suited her to a tee. When I rang her bell, she opened the door a sliver; all I could see was one violet eye and a tousle of blonde curls.

"I wasn't going to open this for anyone, but you're gorgeous!" she purred as she pulled the heavy wooden door toward her, stepping neatly back against the apricot wall. Her hand, with its newly polished half circles of blood, kept fiddling with the belt of her Chinese kimono, and I had the fleeting impression she was going to open it and was figuring, "what the hell" when she smiled. The little teeth gleamed out at me.

I made my explanation short and sweet, turning myself into Beckworth's insurance agent for this go-round. Her interest visibly paled. "Dull" registered behind her appraising little eyes, which was fine with me. We kept it businesslike throughout.

The girl had appeared at about seven, give or take a few minutes, and had still been on the roof when Alison went downstairs. She had said she was waiting for Tom—"Well, she didn't really say it outright," Alison admitted, "but she intimated it—and she had sat down to wait."

Mary and my sixth sense had been right. Alison was an uptight little bitch. I asked her what the other girl had been wearing. She wrinkled up her nose before answering.

"This incredibly old pair of jeans. You'd think she couldn't afford to buy a new pair!"

Jesus! I wouldn't have gone near the blonde with a ten-foot pole, but I tried to charm her with the good ole' McQuade grin anyway. As an insurance agent, it was a safe play.

"Some people are like that." Short pause. "What else was she wearing, do you remember?"

"I don't know. An old white sweater with big holes in it."

"Holes? Moth holes?"

"No. It was the kind of sweater that's made that way. A real large knit. They're made with big needles; you use less yarn that way."

"Could you see through it?"

"Really! What do you think I am?"

"Come on, babe. That's not what I meant. Could you see what she had on under the sweater?"

"Not really. Well, whatever it was, it sure was blue."

Bonanza. I thanked Alison for her trouble and she told me to drop by anytime (probably due to the "babe"). I assured her I would, gritted my teeth, and pushed off. Even if she gave it away it wouldn't be worth it. She was the type who'd gnaw little holes in you until she was satisfied, and she never would be. The fresh air felt great.

Hunter was oiling around the cashiers when I burst into the bank.

"How do you know for sure it's her, Mac?"

"I don't, but I'd be willing to bet on it."

We've played poker together for over ten years now, and Hunter knows when I'm serious. He took out his checkbook.

"You want to go back on payroll, as of today?"

ANTONIA
8.

SOMETHING STRANGE WAS GOING ON, AND I
wasn't sure I liked it. I was changing in ways I didn't
fully comprehend. My adventure at the architect's mansion had gotten me all wired up. It took me hours to fall
asleep that night, and when Rachel crawled into my bed
the next morning, I didn't feel at all tired. I wanted to
go out immediately and buy a paper, to see if anyone
had discovered the robbery. When I thought about the
cold little blonde on the roof, it didn't scare me at all. If
anything, it gave me a little bit of a thrill. Change
number one: instead of worrying about Rachel's future
and mine if I were caught, I was holding my breath,

thinking they'd never catch me—there are too many dark-haired skinny types in San Francisco for them to pin me down.

Rachel and I were horsing around in bed, when I remembered I hadn't typed up the second half of my biweekly paper for Warren, and it was due that day. I poured her a bowl of granola with banana cut into it and a little bit of vanilla yogurt, and she happily munched away while I typed. Suddenly, I realized I was reeling off an average little paper with no difficulty at all. I could follow Warren's bidding and make him totally content—now—and God, it was making life at school easier.

Rachel admonished me for not eating any breakfast myself and finally got up and poured me a bowl of granola. She put in yogurt but no banana, because she isn't allowed to use a knife yet. I've got one great kid.

I bought her a croissant at the Buttercup, and we caught the bus. Rachie wanted to share it with me, but I convinced her it was all hers. On the way to campus, I stopped at a small antique shop to sell the copper kettle. The old man who owns the place likes to bargain. I said $35.00, he only wanted to pay $25.00. We argued back and forth while he dusted antiques. It took a half hour for us to agree on $31.75, so I was a bit late for Warren's class.

Since I'm his T.A., it doesn't look too good when I'm late; but I apologized, explaining how Rachel didn't seem to want to let me go that morning, and within seconds he was mollified. He hesitantly inquired if I had time to grade some papers for him, and when I said, "Of course," he told me to pick them up in his office anytime during the day. I got them on the way to my own office. There was quite a stack of them, but I figured I'd do them that night after Rachie was in bed, if Christopher was willing to come over to study. It wouldn't be much of a hot date, but we would be together.

I dialed his exchange and he picked up right away. He was delighted to hear from me and started to tell me about this great class he had just finished teaching. I couldn't hear too well from my end, because my cellmates were having their usual complaint hour. After a couple of seconds I suggested he come over to study that evening. He told me he'd pick up some ground beef and string beans on the way over, and a bottle of wine.

Teddy and Tom were arguing about some obscure noble's response to the Wars of the Roses, and they were getting quite emotional about it. Leslie added her two cents—"The noble was only standing up for his 'class' rights"—and both men barked at her to stay out of it. She went snuffling off to the ladies' room. As she left, Tom called out, "Why can't you follow Tony's example and mind your own business?" She honked into a Kleenex for an answer and continued on her way.

Actually, I hadn't said anything because I found the whole discussion boring and annoying. Did they care about anything in the real world, any of them, or could they only get heated up over the distant past? That was the second change. I discovered I was becoming very short-tempered with my compatriots, and I figured I had better do something about it since we all had to suffer through at least two more years of each other. It was a relief to walk across campus and down the stairs to the dance building. Seeing those brown shingles covered with ivy perked me up right away. Whatever the reason, I still loved my dance classes. Actually, the reason was becoming a bit twofold. At the bar, my main concern was over my extension: just how far could I stretch my toes with my legs extended? Could I gain an inch or two when I stretched my arm up to the ceiling and my legs straight in front of me, one hand loosely caressing the bar? *Loose* was the key word: it was important in my line of work. Body tension could be hazardous. If I had been scrunched up at the banker's place, I never would have been able to swing the rope aside and clear those balconies.

Jeffrey was delighted with my concentration and the renewed vigor I demonstrated every time I came to class. For the first time in a year, I was no longer skipping a class every few weeks; they were too important to me now—paper number two on the Russian peasant would just have to wait. After class that particular day, Jeffrey drew me aside. I didn't give him a second.

"I'm in a rush, Jeffrey. I don't have time for the Mediterraneum."

He chuckled at me as his arm went around my shoulder.

"My dear Antonia, I have another class to teach, so the café will have to wait for both of us."

"What do you want then?"

Again the chuckle. "I would love to feel free enough to ask you a big favor."

"Come off it, Jeffrey. You're the freest person I know."

144

He loved that.

"The company is giving a concert at Santa Rita tomorrow night."

"Jesus, what a strange place to give a concert." Santa Rita was a prison about fifty miles from San Francisco, in Alameda County.

"Not really, Antonia. We're working with an organization called Artists in Prison, and they've found that doing this kind of thing has been quite successful. I believe it serves as some sort of release for the inmates, as well as bringing them culture they would otherwise be without."

"So?"

"Debbie has the flu. We're doing 'Acrobatic.' You've seen that piece more than ten times. I know if you gave me an hour of your time I could teach you your part quite easily."

I just stared at him.

"Will you do it, Antonia? As a favor to me?"

I was really tempted. Not because of Jeffrey, but because of Santa Rita. What would it feel like to be inside a prison? My stomach was doing flip-flops, but I had some Maalox with me, so that wouldn't be a problem. I was amazed to find myself saying yes.

"Are you free at four? I can pick Rachel up at 5:15, if you'll drop me there."

"Of course, my dear," Jeffrey gushed as he threw both arms around me. "I'll be right here, awaiting your return."

The routine was very easy, and Jeffrey and I were at Wendy's Place by five. Rach wanted to go to the Co-op, but I told her Christopher was coming for dinner. We waved Jeffrey off and walked home. It's not a short walk, but both of us wanted to be outside. Wendy hadn't taken the kids to the park, because she was still nervous about Rachie's arm. We had both tried to assure her it was okay—Rach could swing fine with one arm—but she was guilty and therefore nervous.

Christopher walked in with the groceries at about 7:15, and we both began preparing dinner. I made the hamburgers and cut up the beans while Christopher mashed the potatoes I had boiling on top of the stove. He cut up greens for a salad while he told us about Bill, his favorite student. Whenever Christopher talked about teaching, he gesticulated with his arms and strode around the room, so even Rachel enjoyed the conversation.

"I like Bill," she piped up. "He's okay." We had run into Bill and Christopher walking across campus a few days before.

"What makes him okay, honey?" God, I loved her.

"He's funny. I like the way he laughs at Christopher when he's being all serious and stuff."

Christopher didn't know quite how to take that, but Rach and I laughed and laughed, and finally he picked her up and swung her around the room. We played Botticelli all through dinner, and Rachel was quite good at it. She was pooped and went to bed by eight thirty.

Christopher and I necked like teenagers for a few minutes on the couch and then got down to work. By eleven I had half the papers graded and Christopher had prepared his lectures for Thursday and Friday. He turned on the eleven o'clock news: he watches it every night. I don't usually bother.

146

I was halfway through the next paper before I realized what Van Amberg was talking about. It was the name that got me. "Mr. Beckworth did not discover the theft until the early hours of the morning."

My back shot up, my eyes were riveted to the set. Christopher was listening attentively. I felt my face flush with excitement as the announcer continued describing the robbery, and when he got to the unknown female on the adjoining roof I thought I would die. I knew I should say something, but I just couldn't. After what felt like hours of ominous silence, I blurted out, "Jesus! That's a hell of a place to rob!"

Christopher merely looked at me, very closely, and then he asked me if I wanted a cup of tea. I shook my head yes, and he went into the kitchen.

He knew; I knew he knew. I felt utterly panic-stricken. Christopher was completely aware that I had pulled that job; and if he knew that, he knew I had been lying to him about my activities for over a month as well. The weeks of flu and grading papers. All of it. And that was why I had been feeling like he didn't care for me as much as he had the month before or even the week before. He didn't. It wasn't merely his fear of commitment; it was the added fear of committing himself to who I was becoming. I couldn't bring the whole thing up, because I knew Christopher didn't want to know the truth, straight; plus, I wasn't sure he was the one to tell. As much as I wanted to tell someone about what was happening in my life, I was afraid if I told Christopher he might up and leave me. And that I certainly didn't want.

We had our tea, very quietly kissed a little bit, and

then Christopher picked up his papers and went home. He didn't even argue with me about spending the night, because he didn't really want to. I was confused and sad but didn't know what I wanted to do about it. And the next day was the concert at Santa Rita.

The company drove down in one car, a truck behind carting the lights and costumes and scarves we used in "Acrobatic." There was a little difficulty getting through the main gate—we all had to get out and be searched, while the guard assured us he had to unload the whole truck as well, but it would only take twenty minutes. We all looked around. There were many small cement-block structures dotting the surrounding hills—dorms, I figured—cement walkways, quite a bit of grass, and a strange air of freedom. Which I realized was quite false as soon as my eye took in the chain-link fence, topped by barbed wire, surrounding the whole compound. I had started to shiver. Jeffrey scolded me for not wearing a coat—"Sorry. I don't have one!"—and then lent me his jacket. It hung around my knees and didn't stop the shivering.

By 6:45 we were inside the walls, making our way to the auditorium. Or so we thought. Unfortunately, there was one more checkpoint where we had to go through the whole shebang again.

So of course we were late setting up, late warming up, and late beginning the concert. The prisoners filed in at about 7:45, while Jeffrey and I went through one last number. They hooted and whistled and carried on as if they hadn't seen anything like it in months, or years, and I'm sure they hadn't. They were all female.

I had thought we were performing for the male half

of the prison population and was quite dismayed to discover otherwise. I kept trying to concentrate on learning my routines and getting them down perfectly, but I found my mind and eyes wandering. Several ladies looked like they might even be me: they were slim and dark and attractive and seemed well put-together; I couldn't imagine what they were doing in a place like Santa Rita. Obviously, they had gotten caught.

By the time we went on at 8:15, I had consumed a whole box of Maalox and it hadn't helped a bit. My knees kept shaking and Jeffrey couldn't believe it.

"Antonia, flex your knees and tighten, tighten," he hissed at me in between leaps across the floor.

"I'm trying, I'm trying," I whispered back, and I was. Finally, I half closed my eyes to make it through the hour and a half performance, and by forgetting where I was, I managed to do pretty well. I actually almost enjoyed the last fifteen minutes, which were also the most complex in the show. The applause was deafening.

A prison guard jumped up on stage and announced that there would be a short discussion period with the dancers, but that prisoners 162, 714, and 1018 were due back in cellblock C on the double. There was a lot of hissing and booing as the three women—one black, two Chicana—got up to leave. They were obviously in no hurry to get to cellblock C. It took them a good five minutes to get to the back of the auditorium, accompanied all the way by the catcalls and brouhaha that clearly were a part of prison life.

I felt much less nervous by then and was getting very curious about the ladies in front of me. One of the slim, pretty ones asked me what I did and where I lived, and I told her I was a student at Berkeley with a daughter and that I was only filling in for an ailing dancer. I wanted to tell her I was a burglar, too, but of course I couldn't. Then I asked her what she had done to get inside Santa Rita.

"I got caught selling acid in Berkeley. But I just hung out there. I wasn't a student or anything like that."

She stared very hard at me and I had to turn away. I wasn't telling the whole truth, and I was sure she knew it. Looking back, I know that was crazy; she was just trying to see what the differences were between us—me, the student; her, the prisoner. But that night I was convinced she knew all about me, and it depressed me and made me sad I was becoming dishonest.

Another lady asked Jeffrey if he was gay, and he asked her if she thought all male dancers were, and she said, "Yeah." Then she told him about a gay group that was forming in the prison to petition for equal rights and segregation so they wouldn't be tortured by other prisoners. She let him get by without answering her question; I guess she assumed he was gay, which is a very easy (and accurate) thing to assume about Jeffrey.

One of the other boys in the company asked a short, tough-looking lady in the back how long she had been in prison, and she barked out, "Fifteen months, buddy, with two more years to go. Hey, you," she pointed to me, "your pop seeing you and your kid through school?"

My eyes began to water. Oh, Christ, please leave me alone, I thought. I came to dance and that's all.

"No, I get some money from the university for grading papers, and I'm on food stamps."

She grunted in satisfaction. At least I wasn't part of the coddled middle class. Maybe I seemed okay in her book. I sure as hell didn't in mine.

Actually, I think our group faired terribly in the discussion. We were all uptight and untruthful. Jeffrey couldn't come out and admit to being gay. I lied about how I got money; and Melissa, another girl in the company, refused to answer a couple of pretty personal questions about her life. Luckily Jackie, a black woman, and Lisa, a white one, fit right in and got down to the nitty gritty, so we weren't a total bust. Jackie told one woman she was relieved as hell she could go home but wished they all could too. Pandemonium reigned for a good five minutes. I wished I had had the guts to say that. On the other side, the members of the audience seemed open to anything—hell, what did they have to lose?

None of us talked much on the way home; I went straight upstairs and poured myself a huge glass of wine. What in the hell would I ever do if I got sent to a place like that? I was more relieved than Jackie to have gotten out, and much more scared about being sent back in. How did those women stand it? They had to file out in single lines, and answer any question any guard asked, and do menial tasks during the day to keep busy, and then they just wasted away. One lady told me she had a kid, too—her mother was keeping her till she got out. Oh, Jesus.

Before I went to bed, I made two vows: (1) start being honest with Christopher, and (2) no more robberies.

McQUADE
9.

POUNDING THE PAVEMENT IN SAN FRANCISCO
is a hell of a way to spend a week. I spent one that way,
checking out all the dance shops I had missed on the
first go-round, but came up blank. I was into a heavy
athletic frame of mind, disdaining my cycle, buses, and
cable cars for my own two feet; by the weekend I was
sorry as hell. I was beginning to think I was a rotten
detective, but I couldn't accept the possibility. Maryanne
asked me if we could walk to the theater—we had
worked out an uneasy truce—and I almost punched her
in the mouth. She told me I was foul-tempered; two
bottles of wine didn't help much. By the end of the

evening all she wanted to do was go home. By herself. Some truce.

The next morning a very defeated Mac was ringing Jim Diamond's bell at 10:00 A.M. I was in a hurry to do better and in my zeal forgot that for a guy like Jim, 10:00 A.M. is the middle of the night. It used to be that way for me, too, on weekends anyway, when I worked for Barton, Wells and McDonough, but not anymore. Jim did not look at all pleased to see me, but I didn't give a shit. Pushing past into his understocked kitchen, I put up a pot of coffee, scrambled up some very old-looking eggs, and sat down to talk. Jim looked like he was sleeping sitting up, so I force-fed him. Slowly, oh, so slowly, he started to come back to life.

"What the fuck are you doing here at this hour, McQuade? I should kick you in the balls, you son of a bitch."

"Take it easy, man. You can sleep the rest of the day."

He frowned and passed a hand through his hair. I smiled at him.

"Look, man, you told me to give you a call if I needed any help, and I need help."

"I haven't even seen you in two months, Mac. What the hell are you talking about?"

"The girl, Jim. The girl."

That woke him up. "I thought you gave up on finding her . . ."

"My interest's revived."

"Why?"

"I think she pulled another job."

Jim was quiet for a minute and then he grinned at me. "Beckworth" was all he said.

"How the hell did you know that?"

"I'm in the business, remember? So how can I help you, Mac?"

"I've hit every dance store in San Francisco, Berkeley, and Sausalito, and I need a new pair of shoes. I have gotten to square zero and I'm really pissed off. Do you know how many dark pretty girls there are in this city who dance? Don't ask."

"Why don't you try some of the classier dance studios? Maybe she takes classes someplace."

I was up and halfway out the door before Jim bit off the end of his sentence. I jerked the door open, yelling back, "Why the hell didn't I think of that? Thanks, man. Sleep tight."

On the way over to get my bike, I picked up a yellow pages. The Honda was parked in my old spot at Barton, Wells and McDonough. My name was still stenciled on the cement, and no one ever bothered me there. Leaning up against the wall next to the Honda, I circled the dance studios with the largest ads and decided to start with them. I figured I'd give Alicia, an old dancer-friend of mine, a call that night for the real classy spots and try them on the morrow if the first day's work had been a bust.

The first place I hit was on Polk, near California. The office was upstairs, at the end of a grim-looking hall at the top of a long steep set of stairs. I guess they spent all their bread on advertising: not a classy joint by any stretch of the imagination. The receptionist informed me that each teacher kept his own files, so, to be sure, I'd have to check with everyone. Shit. That meant the whole day at place one. I thought about it and decided to stick. I didn't seem to have much choice. Two of the dance masters were actually pretty nice about it, but three of them were sneering nasty faggots, the kind that lisp at you in the middle of their sarcastic, flip remarks. "You're cute, fella," and that sort of crap. I kept my cool and repeated my spiel. None of them had any students fitting that description. I left my card with the secretary and told her to give me a buzz if a girl fitting the description registered for a class. I didn't feel hopeful about the possibility: the day had been a real drag.

Alicia laughed when I told her about Polk Street—"That place is a real dump, Mac. No one who knows anything about dance would train there!"—but she was surprisingly nice about giving me the right names. There were about seven really *A* places and ten *B* ones. She told me if none of them panned out, she'd think up some more.

"Oh, by the way. There are two in Berkeley that are superfine. Maybe you should try those, too."

I thanked her the only way I knew how. She laughed at her end, telling me she'd be ready by eight on Friday. She assured me I didn't have to, and I assured her I wanted to, so we kept it the way it was: she'd be outside at eight.

The next couple of days were uneventful. I watched about thirty classes while I was waiting around to speak to a bunch of teachers, saw a lot of great tail, and drew a big fat blank. The nights were even worse. The date with Alicia helped some but not that much. She spent whatever remaining strength I had left. But for some reason, by Monday I was raring to go; I got on the bike and headed across the bay at nine.

Climbing the stairs to Cooper's, the second place on my list for the day, I felt a chill go up my spine; maybe this would be the place. Maybe the dance-studio idea wouldn't be a bust. I bounded up the last three steps, running smack into an old buddy on the top landing.

McCracken has been on the force longer than I've been alive, I think. He's old and big and beefy and Irish, and looks just like what a cop should look like. The only shockeroo is that he's smart and soft and a thoroughly nice guy. Honest as can be expected these days. I call him Crackin, and he calls me Mac. He busted the first guy I defended when I got to San Francisco and gave me my first break on the stand. I lost the case anyway, and as far as I know the guy's still in and out of jail; Crackin and I are buddies.

"What's up, man? Your wife takin' up a new way to reduce?"

"Hell, no. She couldn't even make it up those stairs, Mac. What're you doing here? Chasing a bit of the you-know-what?"

I had never lied to Crackin, but I had never had to before.

"Picking up a lunch date. I should've told her I'd meet her outside."

I sat down on the seat next to the cop.

"Is it a bad joint? Are you raiding it?"

"Hell, no. The boss has me on a dumb goose chase again. Some broad in a robbery case was wearing a leotard, so he has me checking out dance studios. Do you know how many girls wear leotards in this town? Christ, I can't believe it."

The sweat beaded up on my lower lip, and I hoped to

hell I looked more nonchalant than I felt. This girl was mine! I didn't want the cops horning in.

"Just be grateful, man. Nothing else looks as fine on a foggy day." I took a breath and tried to look unbelieving. "He really has you looking in dance studios just because the girl was wearing a leotard?"

"God's honest truth. And would you believe that's the only lead we've got? Shit, what a lousy case."

Cool as cool could be, I asked, "Which case, Crackin?"

"Beckworth."

"You gotta be kidding. No lady could've climbed across that roof!"

"You know that and I know that, but not the boss. Hell, no."

A bevy of lovelies swarmed out of the dance studio, and I attached myself to one, telling her I'd meet her downstairs. In a whisper I told her to be cool; I wasn't out to hurt her. I smiled my most dazzling smile. She looked puzzled but didn't say no, and I beat a hasty retreat—nodding and winking to Crackin on the way out.

When the redhead surfaced, I offered to buy her lunch, but she said she had another class to go to across town, smiled, and thanked me.

"I hope you're not in any trouble."

"Nope. Thanks for covering for me."

"It's okay. You've got a nice smile."

I grabbed a quick bite and headed crosstown to another studio. Knowing Crackin the way I do, I knew he'd hit all the places in one area on the same day, and I wanted to stay as far away from him as possible. I worked fast but drew a blank on two more studios. That left only four to go, two in Berkeley.

I couldn't get myself to go out that night. For some reason, the ladycat was really getting to me. I knew she was attractive and bright and agile; I also knew she was a thief. It didn't fit together; but something in my head was getting obsessed with making it fit. I stewed all night, first over the lamb chops and broccoli I fixed myself, and then over a glass of fresh coconut milk. I was beginning to hope that I wouldn't find her; if I didn't, they wouldn't; and if she didn't pull any more jobs, she'd go free.

The next day I was out of the house by eight and in Berkeley by nine thirty. There was an accident on the Golden Gate Bridge, and I got stuck for a good half hour. Someday I am going to drop dead in a car, or on my cycle; not in an accident—I'm too careful—but stuck in a traffic jam or waiting for the carnage of another wreck to be cleared away. Michelle keeps bugging me about being more patient, taking up yoga or some such crap, but I laugh it off. Probably, she's right.

The first studio in Berkeley was a bust but not the second. The receptionist listened to my spiel—slim, dark-haired beauty with large hazel eyes and an olive complexion—frowned with her chin resting in her hand and said, "Yes. I think she does study here, and I'm sure she'll be very glad to get that lost leotard. She doesn't have much money."

Christ, I felt elated. I had found her. Then my stomach tightened into a hard knot. What the hell was I going to do with her? Did I turn her over to Hunter first and let us both grill her? Or did I try it myself first—ask her why she did it, and if her reasons were okay, tell her I'd defend her for nothing after I turned her in. Because I'd have to turn her in, that much I was still sure of. No matter how much Michelle tried to "educate" me, I couldn't dump the law-and-order side of McQuade. It had really dug in and taken hold over the years.

The chubby receptionist stood and headed for the nearest wall.

"I think we have a picture of Beverly in this group here. Yes. Here she is. The third from the left. Her face is a little hidden by Jason, but I think you can see her okay."

I came over on the run.

"Is she the one?" chubs inquired.

My stomach plunged down two stories.

"No. No, she isn't." Too thick in the rib cage, too long in the chin. Not Hunter's type at all.

I beat it and headed for the Mediterraneum for some caffé latte. The studio lead was obviously dead-ending. The only good thing about that was McCracken wouldn't find the little lady either. Why the hell was I feeling so relieved?

I headed back across the bay but did even worse in San Francisco; I didn't get done till after seven. Maryanne was pissed because I was late, so even dinner was dismal. I took her home, and though my heart wasn't in it, bedded her down in her huge king-sized bed. All the while I kept seeing a dark-haired beauty, leaping in the air, but Maryanne seemed satisfied. I was not. Maryanne wasn't even a pleasant diversion anymore. Besides, my little blonde bed-companion was bugging me to go back to B. W. & M., a totally incomprehensible and impossible step as far as I was concerned.

Although joining the public defender's office, or some civil-rights group, had seemed like an absurd idea some months back, it didn't now. I knew I'd like the clients I was defending or, at the very least, find them interesting. By the time I hit the boat, I knew the time had come to move out to greener pastures. Yes, the time had come to bid adieu to Maryanne. The party was definitely over.

Just before I turned out the light, I remember wondering if I was becoming too obsessed with the girl, with my little ladycat.

I didn't do much of anything for a couple of days but putter around the boat. Hunter called to find out how I was doing, and I told him I had drawn a blank but was still thinking about it. On Wednesday, Buz resurrected himself from the dead and came aboard.

"We got real trouble, Mac."

I must have looked wary, because Buz got very uptight, for Buz.

"Don't cop out on us before you even hear what's up. It's your problem just as much as ours, unless you're just living here on a lark . . ."

"Ease up, Buz. The way my face looks has nothing to do with your problem, whatever it may be. I've got plenty of my own and I'm just trying to get clear, that's all."

He slumped into my big easy chair, and I poured him some coffee. He wasn't sure he was ready for it, but he thought he might give it a try if it went with some Sara Lee. I took a bun out of the oven and passed it over.

"So what's up?"

"What's up is they're going to try to kick us out of the marina by August 1."

"I haven't heard anything."

"Job has."

He was the old buzzard who lived in the little ketch out at the end of the line.

"What'd he hear?"

"The fight's over. Everyone who lives within seeing distance is being kicked out."

"Why didn't anyone get hold of me? When I filed those papers, I got the county clerk over to our side . . ."

"Yeah." Buz looked very glum, an unbeliever. He hardly even opened his mouth to speak.

"Michelle and I don't have anyplace else to go. We can't afford to dock the boat one place and live somewhere else."

He took another bun and bit in. He was right. Of all the people I had gotten tight with in the marina, only one guy other than me could really afford to move.

"You have any J & B around, man?"

I shook my head no.

Buz looked like he was going to go on another bender momentarily. I made him a fresh vegetable drink and started to lace up my tennis shoes while he was gulping it down. I asked him where Job had gotten his info, and he said from Mo, the guy who shacks up in the little office on the dock. Mo worked for the opposition, so Mo probably had it straight from the horse's mouth. I sure as hell didn't feel like playing lawyer that day, but I had friends to help.

"Cool out, Buz. I'll find out what I can when I get back from my tennis match."

That seemed okay with him—"A-Okay, Mac. We put our trust in you; you're one sharp dude"—and he lumbered off. I got my racket and balls, strapped them onto my bike, and was off. I was halfway across the bridge before it struck me.

"Real sharp. The little lady I'm after is sharp."

I did a right turn in my head and backed up a minute. The chick took the best pieces Hunter had and some damned nice books as well. Plus she took his special reading lamp. Why the light? Second, she robbed Beckworth. She took some extraordinary pieces from him as well. The lady had class, and she knew how to use it. If I put Hunter and Beckworth together, I had two guys who weren't doing a hell of a lot for society. In some people's books, the little they did do wasn't enough. Maybe that had something to do with why they were hit. Hell, she could be the social-activist type. Whatever she was, she was beginning to add up to a brainy broad with a conscience; and that didn't mean secretary, or clerk, or slouch—it meant school.

"McQuade," I congratulated myself, "maybe you will make a first-rate detective! Screw Maryanne and her disdain for your new line of work, and screw B. W. & M., too."

I burned rubber, zigzagging from lane to lane, in and

out of post–rush-hour traffic. She wasn't just a dancer, if she was even a dancer at all. She was a student, or even possibly a teacher, though that seemed unlikely. Teachers get rotten pay, but they do get paid. By Hunter's guess, she was too old to be an undergraduate—he figured she was in her late twenties—but she could be a graduate student. Maybe in the social sciences, where she'd have to develop concern about good guys versus bad guys. Because without a doubt, she was hitting the guys a social-science professor would label *bad*. He was my old buddy, but Hunter's bank—shit, his bank invested in just about every rotten thing you can imagine. By the time I parked the bike in the club's lot, I was convinced the girl was a student, and probably a social activist, but I didn't say anything to Hunter.

My tennis game was rotten, but Hunter offered to console me with a screwdriver and I couldn't think of an easy way out of it. I made small talk about good tail, gulped down a Virgin Mary, and fled in a little under an hour. The parking lot attendant looked scared shitless as I roared past him out of the lot. I made it to San Francisco State in ten minutes, give or take a few seconds. First I hit the student union, because I knew I would never find the dance department myself in the midst of the maze of buildings. A little lady in horn-rimmed glasses and white cardigan sweater pointed me in the right direction, and a girl in tights, sandals, and a long skirt told me to follow her—"I'm on my way to ballet class over there anyway, mister."

Getting into a conversation with the dance student turned out to be all but impossible. After several attempts at informal conversation, I gave up and decided just to try to find out if she knew "ladycat" instead.

"You been at San Francisco State a long time?"

"Two years. That's long enough."

"You majoring in dance?"

"What do you think?"

She was a real charmer.

"Look. I'm trying to locate a girl. She bought a couple of blue leotards in my shop, paid for them, and then left them on the counter. I figured she might go to school here."

"Why? There are millions of dance studios in San Francisco. She could study at any of them . . ."

Oh no, she couldn't. I had hit all of them.

"Oh, she said something about an exam, so I figure she goes to college someplace."

The girl stopped and looked me over. I'm kind of big, but I keep in shape, and I've developed a tan from working on the boat. My hair is blond, average length, but I've been growing a beard. I had on chinos and a plaid Pendleton.

"You don't look like you own a dance store. All of those guys are gay." She stared me down.

"Okay, you got me." Maybe it was time to revise my story. "I met this chick at a party, but she slipped out on me. I know she studies dance at some college, but I don't know which one."

Old lockjaw was impressed. "You musta really dug her. To be tracking her down at State. What's she look like?"

I went into it, but she stood there shaking her head.

"Nope. She's not at State. We just get the duds here. No one who looks like that'd ever come to State." She grinned up at me, just daring me to refute her.

I tried, mildly, but we both knew I was shucking her. She went smirking off to her class, proud of her victory for some sick reason of her own. I decided to try the office secretary to double-check what the student had said. The secretary was young and reasonably attractive, so I tried the party routine. Mildly disapproving, but impressed, she told me she was sorry to disappoint me, but the oldest student they had was twenty-three and looked nineteen.

"None of our girls are that old." She grinned at me like a co-conspirator. "Or that pretty, for that matter."

I thanked her and turned to go.

"Why don't you try Lone Mountain. It's not too far from here, and you'll still get there before they close down for the afternoon."

"What time is it?"

"It's three o'clock."

I thanked her and split. By three thirty I was pulling into the visitor's parking lot at Lone Mountain. Their dance secretary was an old spinster, very sour-looking, the hair on her upper lip quivering each time she spoke. I switched back to owning a dance store but struck out anyway. She had a tight little voice and very properly informed me that "none of our girls are allowed to wear anything other than your standard black leotard, Mister . . ."

"McQuade."

"McQuade. Why don't you try Berkeley? I hear 'anything goes' over there."

With that she bowed her head over her typewriter, saying a prayer for my safe return from the sin-bed across the bay before she started tapping away at her machine. I thanked her and left.

I was headed for the Bay Bridge when I remembered Buz and the marina. I was worried McCracken knew some things he hadn't told me and might find the girl before I did, but I owed something to Buz. I made a U and headed for a phone booth.

I started to dial old man Barton, thought better of it, and headed over there in person. I looked okay, not great, but okay for a boat freak, and I figured I'd do better for old Buz and me in person. The old man was having his evening round of martinis before heading home, and he poured me one without even blinking.

"You're looking all right, son. Your skin's a good color and I'm glad to see Ida's still pressing your pants."

I watched him sip away and asked him about the business, which I didn't give two shits about anymore: he told me the bare essentials. I think he realized even then how much I had changed over in Sausalito, although I hadn't told him much about what was up. He leaned back into leather, rested both chins on his chest, and rumbled, "So Mac. What can I do for you?"

"Well, sir." I called him that when we were dealing with any serious business. "I think we may have a little problem over in the marina."

The old goat looked at me, waiting for me to finish. He knew I didn't need any prodding.

"The rumors are flying around that Dudley is trying to sell us out. He wants to change the place into a snooty yachting club . . ."

The old man interrupted, quietly. "Like the St. Francis." The yacht club he and his wife belonged to—and me, when I first came to San Francisco, before I discovered it was used mainly by old marrieds and wasn't a good place for a swinging young bachelor to hang out. I grinned.

"Yeah. Just like the St. Francis."

"I would think one St. Francis would be enough for any city." His eyes twinkled at me. I really dug old man Barton.

"So would I, sir." I paused for a second or two, while he poured himself another round.

"You haven't touched your drink, son."

"No, sir. I've given it up."

He didn't bat an eyelash.

"What do you do instead?"

"A little detective work. It's a much finer high."

That made the old man raise his eyebrows but no more.

"I'll see what I can find out for you, son. Give me a call tomorrow after two."

He finished his drink, chatted a bit about his wife and daughter, and held the door for me. His Rolls was waiting; I followed him out on the Honda. I think he would have preferred riding with me.

Buz was disappointed I didn't know anything for sure but promised not to go on another bender before I got the word. I wanted him to help me plan a course of action. I turned in early because I planned on being in Berkeley by ten at the latest.

Michelle and Buz came by for breakfast, so I was a

little later getting started than I had expected—I didn't even push off until 10:15. By eleven thirty, I had nosed around the student union and been directed to the lower level and a small, brown-shingled building. Somehow it was a very pleasing sight, nestled in between the imposing concrete slabs that house the various departments that make up UC Berkeley.

No one was in the office when I arrived, except a very little girl with long blonde hair tied up in blue ribbons, who was lying in the middle of the foyer floor, reading a Dr. Seuss book.

"Hi. The lady who sits over there'll be back in a minute. She went to the bathroom."

With that she was done with me and back into her book. Indeed, the dumpy little middle-aged receptionist did return in a minute, and I went into the party bit. Quietly. Somehow, I didn't want the kid to hear me; the whole idea was embarrassing.

The receptionist apologized: "I've only been here about three months, and I don't really know everybody all that well. Why don't you wait for the twelve o'clock dance class to let out and ask Jeffrey. He's been here for five years, so he might know if the young lady attends Berkeley or not." She motioned me over to the set of plastic orange chairs behind the little girl. Obediently, I sat down to wait.

"Rachel. Would you like a cookie!" The receptionist was standing by the wooden fence that separated her from us, with a box of ginger pogens in her paw. The kid jumped up and took two. She said thank you immediately and sat down with the cookies.

"Would you like one of my cookies? My mommy loves them. She says they're almost as good as chocolate ice cream."

"It's okay. You can have them."

She was obviously very relieved to be able to keep them for herself.

"I'm waiting here for my mom to get out of class. Wendy's got the flu."

"Who's Wendy?"

She struggled for the right word. "My ... um ... teacher."

"Nursery school?"

Her mouth was already filled with a crumbled pogen, but her bangs bounced as she nodded a vigorous yes. Somehow the kid made me feel like smiling. She was a winner.

"Is your mom a dancer?"

She finished one cookie and held the other close to her mouth.

"Sort of. She studies other stuff, too. What do you do?"

"I'm a lawyer." I wanted to keep it simple.

She shook her head, satisfied; in went the cookie, and her attention returned to the pictures in the Dr. Seuss book. Every now and then she'd chuckle out loud or ask me to read her a sentence or two, but by and large she kept to herself. She was direct and chipper and quite unpolished; I liked her. By 12:15 I was beginning to feel impatient. Rachel nudged my knee.

"It's okay. Jeffrey's class usually runs over. They should be out any minute."

And, by God, the door opened seconds later and a few lithe-looking dancers ambled out. I had definitely developed a thing for dancers over the past few months. Their bodies are so damned supple, their tits so firm-looking. I even love the way they walk, with their toes out, shuffling off down the hall in their ballet slippers. About ten girls left the room and that was it. None of them had black hair. After about two or three seconds, a tall man pranced out, talking animatedly with a slim dark beauty in a black leotard. I almost stopped breathing. The kid leaned on my knee and leaped up, shouting, "Mommy! Mommy! Hurry up. I'm hungry. Can we get some falafel on the way home?"

The lady bent over in one beautiful motion, scooped up the kid and her book, and continued on down the hall. I watched her dig a sandwich out of her canvas bag before the child could overwhelm her with talk about her book and the events of her day, including her short conversation with me. I resisted the impulse to go after the mother to tell her what a lovely kid she had, and turned to follow the instructor instead.

He listened to my tale rather impatiently and about halfway through started to smile.

"You really want to find her, don't you? She your dream girl, lover boy?"

I kept it cool. "Maybe so. All I know is I've gotten obsessed with finding her."

I seemed to do okay under his appraising eye.

"Yeah, well, I don't think your girl goes to Berkeley. The only one I know who even vaguely resembles her is Tony." He pointed after the young mother. "But she doesn't go in much for parties. She's not the type. Besides, if Tony had been the girl at your party, you'd be talking to her now and not me, right?" With that he turned to the receptionist, calling over his shoulder, "Sorry," before he handed her his attendance book.

I watched the young graceful beauty retreating down the hall, her back and arms hardly even affected by the forty or so pounds she was carrying. My stomach lurched forward and I felt very sorry I had had that second helping of pancakes for breakfast. All I could think of was Hunter's *Winnie-the-Pooh* book. My head started shaking the *no* involuntarily. It couldn't be her.

ANTONIA
10.

CHRISTOPHER AND I HAD WORKED OUT AN
uneasy truce: by the summer we were enjoying each
other again and enjoying swimming and boating with
Rachel. Life was full and very busy. Wendy vacationed at
Stinson Beach for a week in July, and on days when
Nicole's mother couldn't take Rach to the park or to the
beach, she came to class with me. I loved bringing her
along; she added color to the drab surroundings. Professor Warren had gotten some money for the
summer—about nine hundred dollars for two and a half
months—and I was supposedly doing research for him.
He was in a fallow period, so there was very little to do
for the money.

Rachel sat in on my Modern Russia course once and had also endured a lecture on how to do research, in my research seminar—boring, boring! Much to my surprise, she was developing an overwhelming appetite for anything Russian, and I was having a hell of a time finding books she could understand, to quell her hunger. Obviously, Warren had no idea what to suggest; all he knew were monographs and the like for harried graduate students. I found a little picture book on Russia at Mo's, which Rachie devoured the second time she went to class with me.

Afterward, Professor Warren asked me if I had a minute to talk to him. I pointed to Rach, totally absorbed in the book, and he said that was okay, so all three of us traipsed off to his little alcove.

"You have quite a mommy, young lady!"

She solemnly shook her head at him, sat down, opened her book, and continued reading.

"Antonia, you are the best student I have had in over five years. In the beginning you were a bit absent-minded and your papers were not terribly disciplined, but in the past six or seven months you have positively blossomed. You're starting to concentrate and it shows."

"Thank you." What a schmuck. I had stopped thinking when I wrote them, and that was what he called "blossoming."

"Have you given any thought to what you might do for your dissertation?"

"Not really. I still have quite a bit of course work to do."

"No, you don't. With the courses you are taking

this semester, and a slightly heavier load in the fall, you could start on your research by the spring quarter."

"I didn't realize that . . ." It really was a shock. I wasn't prepared to do any research and hadn't even thought about a topic, let alone chosen one. School was something I still did every day because of Rachel. It gave me plenty of time to spend with her, when I wasn't pulling a job, and the possibility of doing so forever and ever, once I was teaching. I had been doing okay and even had hopes that I would make it through to the Ph.D. and my own salvation. The only problem I had was not being able to keep myself from thinking about my sideline and feeling proud of how proficient I had gotten at it. I was a fantastic cat burglar. I had pulled four jobs, two of them actually very dangerous, and never been caught, except by Christopher. My hauls had been impressive and would have been more so if I could have figured out a way of getting a larger bag away from each spot.

"Tony? I hope I haven't shocked you too badly? . . ."

"Oh, no. I was just thinking about being an actual doctor. Ph.D." It was so weird. I mean, being a cat burglar wasn't something I should have been feeling proud of.

"Well, my dear, if we can decide upon a thesis topic, you may be one even sooner than you anticipate. You have become a very quick researcher-writer, among other things."

"Do you have any ideas on what might be a good period for me to look into, sir?" The words rolled right out of my mouth. After all, I no longer gave much thought to what I was doing at school, and, hell, it was easy to ask the question he obviously wanted me to ask. Furthermore, if he chose the topic, he'd be more disposed to help me with it and like it when I was through. The whole process might only take a few months; then I'd be able to get my life together.

"How did you enjoy the two monographs you read on the Decembrist movement?"

"Very much. I thought they were relevant, especially in terms of what's going on today in this country."

Another example of the difference in our thought processes. Both books had been required reading for him over twenty-five years ago; and although they were pre-Freud, he believed I should still read them. Discipline was a good thing, and he was sure the books had something to offer, even if some of them were a "trifle" boring. My God! Where was he coming from, and, more important, where could he ever go?

"Then I think you should consider buying these four books."

With that he handed me a little handwritten piece of paper. Three of the books were in Russian, one was in German. All were expensive.

"I know you're a bit hard up, Antonia, but perhaps your parents might be willing to help you with it. It is a worthy cause, you know. Dr. Weiner. Don't you think they'd be proud of that?"

I merely stared at him, feeling my annoyance grow. When he looked down, I managed to answer, "I'll try."

After all, how could he possibly understand anything else?

Warren nervously began collecting his papers, put on his glasses, and sat down.

"Well, yes. Why don't you think about it for a few days and then decide what you want to do . . ."

With that he bent over his papers and set to work. I nudged Rachel, who had been totally silent all this time, and edged her out of the room; we sat down in the hall so she could tell me about what she had been reading and show me a picture or two. Then we grabbed the No. 51 home. I couldn't keep from ruminating all the way there about how "well" I would have done as a graduate student if I had cared at all about what I was doing. And how much better if I had expressed any of that caring or any of what was *me*.

After I put Rachel to bed that night, I sat down in my only really comfortable chair, took my shoes off, put my feet up, and started to read about Stalin's prison camps. I couldn't concentrate. For some reason my mind kept wandering back to that dance concert I had given at Santa Rita; in particular I kept picturing the dark, pretty slim woman who had asked me what I did when I wasn't dancing. Why had I lied to her?

I got up and poured myself a glass of Almadén. What do you mean, dummkopf? You lied because you couldn't very well tell her the truth. If you had, you and old "slim" would probably be roommates.

What the hell was happening to me? I poured more wine. Crime was wrong. Criminals were people I read about in the paper and didn't think much about afterward, and now I *was* one. I, Antonia Weiner, future teacher, was a criminal. I could become that girl's roommate. Where would that leave Rachel?

Maybe I should volunteer to run dance workshops in Santa Rita with Jeffrey. He'd been bugging me to join him for weeks now and couldn't understand why I kept refusing.

"After being in there even once, Antonia, can't you see how desperately we're needed? How can you be so heartless?"

Indeed, how could I? I took out Warren's booklist and decided to stop fooling around. I knew why I was thinking about Santa Rita. There was only one way I would be able to pay for those books.

On the way to my office I stopped at Cody's. They had two of the books in stock, but the girl told me they'd have to special order the other two. The bill: $215.75. I asked her to repeat it.

"What do you mean it'll cost two hundred fifteen dollars and seventy-five cents? How the hell can any books cost that much? There are only four of them!"

Her boss looked up from his paperwork.

"What can I tell you, lady? The two books we have to order, have to be special ordered from New York, and New York has to special order them from Germany. One costs seventy-five dollars and the other sixty dollars. Then there's the mailing costs, etc. With the other two books, it comes to"—he looked down at his pad and totaled it up—"two hundred fifteen dollars and seventy-five cents. I'm sorry, but that's the way it is." He paused and looked at me. "You still want me to order them?"

"Yes." I turned on my heel and exited. Of course I did. I wanted to write the damned dissertation and be done with it. I wanted to do it the easiest and quickest way possible, by doing exactly what Warren wanted me to. Then I could quit that and become a creative teacher. I could. I stopped in the middle of Telegraph Avenue.

"Come off it, Tony. That's not why you're going to pull this job."

"No?" I answered myself. "Then why am I?"

"To spice up your life. You like figuring out a plan and executing it. Those books give you a perfect excuse."

I was horrified. Because it was true. Yeah, I would be nice to get the doctorate and be able to teach. But if I was going to be honest, I no longer knew if teaching could be for me what it was for Christopher. Now.

Oh, my God. Christopher. Christopher was going to be a real problem. I hadn't lied to him in months, and we had been doing very well. Of course, there hadn't been anything to lie about.

And damn it, there still wasn't! If Christopher and I were ever going to make it, I had to share all of my life with him. No matter how I had changed, duplicity was still not my style; I wasn't going to take that path. Maybe if I got into all the why's and wherefore's of my current occupation with Christopher, it would all get straightened out somehow.

All the way to campus I thought about it. I thought

about what Christopher would say if I told him the truth. He wouldn't like it. Not in a million years. But I didn't really like it either. It was just more interesting than Cal, and I could explain that to him thoroughly. We could talk honestly about how we both felt about it and see if we could come up with another solution.

Christopher would love that; it's just his style—to systematically look for answers to every problem. Okay, so we'd look. There was the part-time job possibility, but that wouldn't work because of Rachel. There was the possibility of our living together. That wasn't a bad idea. It would cut down my rent—his place did have two bedrooms, so Rachie and I could move in without much hassle. We could rearrange his living room so both our desks fit; maybe even design a wall unit on the wall by the window. With the $135 I saved in rent, I could even switch over to German history; start over with Professor Gelb. Or I could take a breather and figure out what I could do that would give some meaning to my life and enhance the world at large as well. Given half a chance, I could go back to being Don Quixote. What the hell, I could let Christopher support me for a while. . . . How did I feel about being kept? Not great, but living with someone isn't really being kept. We'd be trying to build a relationship. If we wanted to get married eventually, we could. I didn't think Christopher was ready yet, and neither was I. The first step was to straighten out how I was starting to feel about school and everything else, so we could start in a real place. Okay. I would tell him the truth.

That afternoon after my class I walked over to Barrows Hall. His office was in the basement, down a long dingy hall almost at the end, on the right. He had livened it up with a Mexican rug and a splashy print on the wall above his desk; the other walls were lined with bookcases.

The room always smelled liked Balkan Sobranie, and I loved to sit there and read. It was a comforting oasis in the midst of the Berkeley monolith. I peeked in, not wanting to disturb Christopher if he was with a student, but there he was, in his imitation Eames chair, pipe lit, reading *Foreign Affairs*. He didn't even hear me. I threw a package of raisins across the room; they landed in his lap. Christopher was startled, but as soon as he saw me his face broke into a grin.

"Well, hello. I didn't think I was seeing you until tomorrow night."

I closed the door behind me and sat on his lap.

"Well, hello! I wanted to see you today."

I opened the box of raisins and popped a few in his mouth. He loved it when I did things like that. He said it made him want to bite my fingers, one by one, and go on from there.

"You are a little devil. Ms. Devil."

I kissed him long and hard and got off his lap. As I was pulling over his desk chair I spoke out, loud and clear.

"I need to talk to you, Christopher."

"It sounds serious."

"It is."

"Okay. Shoot."

"I might not be able to see you tomorrow night or the night after that either."

His back got stiff. "Why not?"

I just stared at him a minute before even opening my mouth.

"Come on, Christopher. You know why not."

"No, I honestly don't."

"I have to buy some special books for my dissertation research. They'll cost me two hundred and fifteen dollars."

Christopher didn't say anything.

"There's no other way I can get the money, Christopher."

Christopher stood up and walked over to his desk. He started to bang the base of his pipe against the ashtray and set to cleaning it systematically and then refilling the damned thing. Finally he turned around.

"Why don't you get a part-time job?"

"Because I'd never get to be with Rachel."

Christopher flushed; he was getting angry.

"So you'll see her a little less. She'll live."

"We have different priorities, Christopher."

"Maybe if you didn't spend so damned much time with her, Rachel would be a little less spoiled."

"What does the word *spoiled* mean, Christopher? Overloved? Overfed? Overplayed-with?"

"Spoiled means spoiled, and that's what she is."

"Don't get nasty just because she prefers playing ball to working on Creative Playthings puzzles."

Neither of us spoke for several minutes. The silence was very uncomfortable. Christopher sat on his desk and began rubbing his eyes with his hands. This conversation was not going the way I had thought it would.

"Do you like doing it, Tony?"

"I don't know. It's very strange, but I feel proud that I've learned to do it as well as I have."

"Jesus Christ!"

"I'm sorry, Christopher. I'm trying to be honest with you and sort it all out."

"Oh, Tony." He looked genuinely troubled, and I'm sure he was. "Why don't I give you some money."

"I can't take it. I thought I could when I was coming over here, but I can't. Michael always made such a big deal over every penny. It wouldn't be a good thing for us to get into a situation like that, where I'd be so dependent on you."

Nothing came out sounding right, but I didn't know how to start over, how to explain my own turmoil honestly. I kept censoring this and that, so I wouldn't turn Christopher off, and that just seemed to be making everything worse.

I didn't know what else to say. Christopher was looking out the window.

"Would you marry me if I asked?"

"Are you asking?"

He didn't answer; I knew we were stalemated. Christ, it was over. I picked up my books and slung my pocketbook over my shoulder. Then I leaned up in back of Christopher and kissed him on the shoulder.

"Good-bye."

I turned and ran from the room and down the hall and out of the building and all the way to the bus. I didn't stop crying till I got to Wendy's Place.

So. That was the end of Christopher.

McQUADE
11.

BY MID-JULY I HAD THE RIDE TO BERKELEY
down to thirty-five minutes. I had my own little parking
spot on Benvenue, and the counter guy at the Mediterraneum and I had become buddies. Buz and old man
Barton had talked the Marina West people into the necessity of a more secluded spot for the kind of clientele they
had in mind and were scouting locations together. They
dug each other. The old codger had unearthed
credentials no one knew Buz had: three years of medical
school—Johns Hopkins—a love of healing, and a hatred
of business, any kind. A dropout, like me. Things were
shaping up all around.

The girl had been under constant surveillance (by me) for almost a month and had done absolutely nothing out of the ordinary. I hadn't seen McCracken since I had left him at the dance studio on Polk a month before, so I was assuming his boss had given up on finding a dancer. But I had enrolled in a marine biology class at Berkeley so that I had a real reason for being there, just in case Crackin should come nosing around. I wasn't sure whether I didn't want him to know we were more than likely tracking the same lady (who had committed two crimes, not one) or if I just wanted to be around in case he found her, so I could lend a helping hand should she need it.

This particular week, my lady—following her so obsessively all month really had made her seem like she was mine—was taking her little girl to school with her. They came on campus equipped with Dr. Seuss books, crayons, paper, and simple puzzles; the child sat outside reading or drawing or talking to the department secretary while her mother went to class. She was a very self-sufficient little kid; I liked her more and more. If I ever got married and had children, I hoped they'd be like her.

Actually, I think I began thinking at around the same time that if I ever got married, the lady would have to be a lot like the kid's mother. She had really gotten to me. Her energy level was extraordinary, as was her concentration. Every day she attended two or three classes, picked up papers or books or some other kind of work from the professor she worked for, played with the little girl on the lawn, shopped at the Co-op, cooked, cleaned, put the kid to bed, and presumably sat down to study after I was long gone in Sausalito, eating my salad and preparing for a healthy night of sleep. Three days a week she taught a dance class to little eight- or nine-year-old girls and at least twice a week spent several hours huddled over her books in an alcove at the library. To top it off, she munched a thick strand of health-food licorice while she studied. Black. My favorite kind.

One afternoon I sat at the desk across the stacks from her and tried to read; but after about an hour, I had to give up. All I really wanted to do was look at Tony. Her name was Tony. Antonia. And she was more beautiful than Hunter could possibly have noticed, let alone described to me, in the short time he had had to look at her. Her dark hair had streaks of auburn in it and was thick and luxurious. When she danced, she piled it on top of her head, but most of the time she wore it loose, and it swooped down across her shoulders and ran down her back. The back was lean and straight and slim and looked as smooth as the skin of a tender young peach. The front was delectable. Small firm tits, with nice firm nipples. Little mound of tummy, round long thighs—Christ!—she had really gotten to me, even without her eyes. With them I knew I was lost. They were large and round, and inquisitive and hazel, the most magnificent eyes I had ever seen. They were definitely not the eyes of a criminal.

She read without looking up once and never even noticed me. On one hand, that was for the best, of course. On the other, I wouldn't have minded being

187

noticed—and appreciated. I'm big and well put-
together and have never had a very hard time finding a
lady to do just that. They like me; why shouldn't she?
Was I too square? Not anymore, I told myself. There
was the beard and the boat and the fact that I was almost
poor. I had gone off Hunter's payroll again, having informed him I had drawn another blank. I had sunk my
savings into some long-term investments, so I was running pretty short of cash. I didn't give a damn. I was
really enjoying myself.

"Hey, you've got my ball!"

I looked down and discovered I was holding a red
rubber ball. It was the little girl's. She and I were both
sitting on the lawn outside the dance studio. She was
playing catch with herself, and I was watching her
mother teach a class.

"Sorry." I threw it back and she caught it. "Hey,
you're pretty good."

"I'd be even better if I had someone to play with . . ."

Why not, I thought, and held up my hand so she'd
throw the ball back. I was still able to keep one eye on
the classroom and one on the child. She ran and dived,
and jumped around the ball, and threw it damned
straight for a little kid. Much to my surprise, I realized I
was having a very good time with her. It was good to get
a little exercise. However, when the little girls inside
began crowding around her mother, I handed the ball
back to the kid, tousled her hair, and thanked her for
the game.

"I've got to go to class, kid. See ya around."

"I'll be here again on Friday. My mom teaches a dance class then, too."

She wanted me to come back so badly, it made me a little sad. Where the hell was her father? Why didn't he play catch with her? The kid had lots of friends—I had watched her day-care group play in the park a couple of times—but this was something else entirely. For some totally fool reason, the kid was making me feel needed.

I beat it fast, before her mother came out to join her, and watched them tumble around in the grass from the steps a little way off. From far away they both looked so tiny and fragile and innocent.

It couldn't be her.

Friday I got there a little late because I wanted to make sure Tony was already inside teaching her class. The child was hunched over on the grass, very intent on something. She was coloring, not in one of those books with the pictures all planned out, but on a huge plain piece of construction paper. The picture was free-form, but you could make out grass and a tree and several enormous birds.

"Hey, I like that, kid. What kind of birds are they?"

"Singing birds. I hear them in the morning when I wake up."

She didn't even look up; she had clearly been expecting me. Her outfit was well suited to her. She had on bright yellow shorts and a yellow and red Mexican blouse. Her hair was pulled back in two separate clumps and tied with orange ribbon. Her eyes were smiling and she was very busy.

"I forgot my ball. What's your name?"

It was all run together and said in one breath.

"It's okay, kid. I brought a softball because I think you're good enough to play catch for real. My name's Mac."

"That's a funny name, but I like it."

She sat up and looked at me. She was on the verge of something.

"Do you really think I'm good enough?"

"I sure do. Come on. Let's play."

I pulled her to her feet, and for fifteen minutes we threw and ran and jumped and generally horsed around. By that time, she had really gotten the hang of it and could catch it every time I threw it right to her. She threw it back high and short, but with great energy, and her little ponytails flopped and shook along with her whole body. She laughed with absolute glee every time I missed it. When I started to go, she tugged at my arm.

"Don't go, Mac. I want you to meet my mommy. Couldn't you stay a minute more? She'll be right out, I know she will."

"Sorry, Rachel. I have a class. See you soon."

I felt a pang, leaving, because I really didn't want to, but I reminded myself I was on a job, and I beat it. Although I wasn't working for Hunter anymore, I believed I was working nonetheless. I had to, except toward what end I no longer knew. Law-and-order McQuade wasn't as tough as he had been a month before. Actually, my whole life felt a little out of whack, upside down, but I kept slugging. The blind leading the blind.

A couple of days later I had actually gone to my own class and was heading across campus to try and find Tony. She didn't teach that day, and her history class got out at the same time mine did. I figured I'd find her in the library, because it was her day to go there. I was crossing the bridge on my way to Dwinelle when I saw the kid, sitting by the wall, crying.

"Hi, kid. What's up?" I put my arm around her.

"I can't find my mommy."

"Where is she supposed to be, honey? Do you know?"

"In her office. She told me to wait outside, but I started to play this game with a beautiful blue bird, and then I was here and I couldn't find her."

She had stopped crying and was nestling her head on my shoulder.

"Do you know the name of your mommy's building, Rachel?"

She shook her head no. And started crying again.

"Hey sport, cut it out. We'll find her. It'll be okay." It felt good holding her.

"What does she study?"

"This." She shoved a book into my hand. The book was called *Tina Goes to Russia*.

"You sit right here, and I'll find out where the Russian Department is. I'll be right back."

Of course I knew where the building was, and Tony's office in particular, but I had to pretend I didn't, which made me feel like a louse. I didn't like lying to the kid;

she was so straightforward. Like her mother must have been. I loped back across the plaza and grabbed her hand and raced her down the steps and around a corner to Dwinelle. As soon as she saw the building, her whole face lit up.

"That's it. That's where I'm supposed to meet her. I go inside and it's right down the stairs in the basement!"

I let go of her hand and pushed her up the stairs to the front double door of Dwinelle.

"Aren't you coming with me, Mac? Please."

"I'm sorry, honey, but I can't. I'm already late for a class."

She was a very accepting little person.

"Okay. Will you come play ball with me on Monday?"

"I'll be there. I'll bring the softball and maybe a mitt this time, okay?"

I will never forget the sight of that small yellow blob grinning down the stone steps of Dwinelle at me. For the first time in months I felt like a bona fide louse.

ANTONIA
12.

IT LOOKED LIKE AUGUST WAS GOING TO BE A very good month. A couple of nights after I decided to pull another job, to pay for the books, I was leafing through the *Wall Street Journal* when I noticed the West Coast branch offices of ARCO were having a conference in Boston with the East Coast offices in the middle of the month. Something about ARCO rang a bell; I went through my files. Sure enough, my businessman, James Harris, was a VP in the San Francisco office. I called his office, posing as an old friend from back East (he was born in Philadelphia) who would be in town in a week— "I want to surprise him, you know. We haven't seen each other since high school." His secretary sounded genuinely chagrined when she informed me Mr. Harris would be out of town for that week and the week after it, as well. Could she tell him who was calling? I sounded equally chagrined and then got cheerier. "Oh no." Dramatic pause.

"But maybe I could switch my vacation around a little bit so I wouldn't miss him. Don't even tell him anyone called, okay?"

Okay said she, already a co-conspirator.

The next job was to check out his house. As luck would have it, his brownstone was on one of those lovely little alleys you find in Knob Hill—all green and planted, with back porches and trestles and the like. His was the third house in from the corner. If anyone were sitting on the stoop of the corner house facing the street, they could peer around and see the façade of Harris's place. That didn't seem very likely: it would be a good hit. His particular building had no fire escape. The first-floor windows had no ledges to speak of and were pretty far from the ground. The second story had a large bay window, and the third, two smallish windows with wide ledges. If I could get up there, I could crouch down and crawl in one of the windows. It was very chancy, especially if the windows were kept locked. I would have to find a way into the house.

I worried about that for a few days—Rachel thought I was depressed because of Christopher—and then it came to me. I donned a very chic Chanel suit my mother had bought for me when I went off to college (she knew nothing about Antioch and was quite upset when I came home every Christmas in the same jeans and work shirt, minus the fancy suit) and hitched across the bridge in under an hour. By eleven in the morning, I was ringing Harris's bell. His live-in maid opened the door after the third ring in her crisp little black uniform with starched white collar and apron.

"Yes? Can I help you?"

I smiled brightly. "I certainly hope so. I am conducting a survey of the immediate vicinity for San Francisco International Airport. Due to some testing we may be doing of a new type of passenger liner, it is imperative that we check the type of windows installed in all the houses in this immediate neighborhood."

I kept smiling and waited patiently. She caught on within seconds.

"Why, of course. Won't you come in?"

I went from window to window, floor to floor, hammering with a tiny mallet I had brought along for the purpose, taking down little notations here and there (actually writing down what was around and easily portable, in my own cryptic shorthand), until I reached the third floor. I spent a little longer there, and frowned and humphed and made a show of it. Finally, after about ten minutes, or what certainly felt like it, the maid excused herself—she had some dusting to do downstairs and did I mind? After she left, I took out a small penknife and broke the lock on one of the little windows. Then I fixed it so that no one would notice, unless they were looking awfully closely or were trying to open the window itself. The room didn't seem to be used very frequently; it had a daybed, empty chest of drawers, and small night table (very dusty), and that was all, so my chances seemed good. Hopefully, no one would touch the window for a few days.

I hastened up to the fourth floor, hammered around, made some discrete noise, and then came back down. Thanking the maid politely, I told her I thought all their windows were quite sound.

"We may have to put in some new glass on the fourth floor, but that's all. Would it be convenient for us to come back anytime, if the chief engineer does think it necessary?"

"Oh yes. Well, Tuesday might be a problem. It's my day off. But I'm sure Mr. Harris wouldn't mind changing it to Monday if you need me here on Tuesday."

Bonanza. I wouldn't even have sitter problems.

"Oh no. Any day. Monday through Friday would be fine with us. We'll give you a call tomorrow if we have to do the work. Thank you so much."

We shook hands and she let me out. I had a coffee and bun on Market Street and then made my way to the stores. Getting into Harris's house was going to take some fancy maneuvering: I would have to climb up the building—three floors' worth—open the jimmied window, and slide through. I didn't want to chance leaving by the front door, so I would have to shimmy back down the rope and leave by the alley when I was done. Coming down wouldn't be so bad—hell, I had swung down Hunter's building the last two floors, and then I was fifteen floors above street level—but climbing up would be tricky. I had never done anything like it.

My ballet shoes wouldn't do for this kind of job; I

would need shoes that would grip a wall. So I went into the first store I came to, not my old standby, and bought a fifteen-dollar pair. Then I walked around for a while. It's good exercise for my legs, and I tend to think best when I'm walking. I had a whole evening to plot out; my stomach was hopping around, my feet were jittery, and my head was excited. I was good and I knew I could do it. I caught a trolley to Ghirardelli Square because I had a sudden urge for a hot fudge sundae.

That turned out to be a bad mistake. While I was eating it I began to feel a little bit nauseated. A man was sitting at a table by the window who looked very familiar. My mind started clicking a mile a minute, but I couldn't quite place him. Maybe he had been following me. Maybe he knew what was what. Christ, I asked myself over and over, where had I seen him before?

No matter how hard I wracked my brain, I could not remember. He saw me staring and grinned a toothy grin. Then he winked. My God, I didn't know him! He was just after an easy pickup. I felt relieved, but I had been so freaked by my own paranoid thoughts that I couldn't finish the sundae. I got up, ordered some ice cream for Rach, and split for Berkeley.

Rachel was in a marvelous mood when I picked her up. The whole group had spent the day in the park playing ball, or Rachel had been playing ball with a friend while everyone else swung on the swings, and she was really exhilarated. When they got back to Wendy's, everyone had been so exhausted that they took a nap. Rach gave up her naps when she was a little more than two, so I couldn't believe my ears. She assured me that she, too, had slept, and that it had been very nice, although she felt "awful grouchy" when she woke up.

"My mouth tasted ucky and my eyes kept getting stuck, so I don't think I'll do it too often, Mommy."

So much for mommy's fantasies. We had cold chicken for supper and ice cream for dessert topped with sprinkles and maraschino cherries, and then we went out for a short walk. About two blocks from the house we ran into Christopher. It was very awkward, although it could have been worse. He could have been with a girl.

When I saw him coming toward us, my heart started going like mad and I wanted to run, but I didn't know which way to go. Rach was too busy missing the cracks in the sidewalk to notice him, and then she said very cheerfully, "Hello, Christopher." She added, "I'm sorry," and continued to count the cracks on Christopher's piece of cement. Kids can be so damned cryptic.

"I'm sorry, too, Rachel. I've missed our Botticelli games; maybe I'll come by some Saturday soon and we can play."

Rachel turned and grinned, "C."

Christopher ruffled her hair, "That couldn't be Cookie Monster, could it?" All the while looking at me.

Reaching out to me through my daughter seemed perfect. It was Christopher's way of trying out "can we be friends" and letting me take the ball and run with it or not. He looked so expectant and dear and earnest that I couldn't be angry anymore. "This Saturday would be okay, in the afternoon." We arranged to meet near the marina at two. Christopher waved his good-bye, turned the corner, and was gone. I still did care for him, even if we weren't an ideal couple.

I suppose I always knew, instinctively, that we couldn't have made it. Christopher's too sincere and serious, and I'm changing too fast. Who knows what or who I'll need, or who would even want me. I don't mean to be pejorative about myself, but taking on a lady criminal/graduate student/dancer-with-child demands a very particular sort of guy, although what kind of particular I'm not quite sure of. Maybe just someone who's open. Now Christopher is kind and considerate, but he is certainly not open. I think he's too dedicated to be open. It *was* sad.

And so I continued my preparations. I worked very hard in dance classes and in my spare time worked out at the bar to strengthen my leg and arm muscles. I didn't bother staking out the house, because I knew when the maid would be gone and I knew Harris was out of town. It was pleasant for once, not to follow some boring stud around San Francisco, and made the whole job seem terribly easy.

There was no way to practice climbing up, because I didn't really have time to go back to the Sierras, so I had to trust my instincts. Actually, the idea of being daring, and doing something I wasn't totally prepared for physically, made me quite excited. It wasn't dangerous in terms of my getting caught, because no one would be around. The house on the left of Harris's was vacant and up for lease; and the other jutted out a little, so if anyone looked out the window they couldn't see the back of the building I'd be climbing up. If I fell it would hurt—I suppose if I fell from the third floor it would more than hurt—but I knew I could do it, and the challenge was well worth it. It was certainly better than writing another biweekly paper.

That was precisely what was making me uneasy in my soul. I knew, I really knew, that the actual reason I was pulling the Harris job was for the excitement and for the pleasure of planning and actually executing it. Sure, I needed the books and had no other way of paying for them. Given my situation, I had no choice but to become a Ph.D. But. And it was a big but. In my gut I was relieved to have an excuse for pulling another job. And that terrified me, because it meant I was a full-fledged criminal.

Could I ever go back to the Antonia Weiner I had been at Antioch—that "truly creative" intellect who was a "natural" candidate for teaching? I had really liked that person; but I wasn't sure I even wanted to be friends with who I was becoming, and I didn't like that. To top it off there was Rach, and I certainly felt responsible for her. I told myself it was time to think about quitting and made the promise that I'd give some real thought to my overall problem—what to do for money and with my life—after I hit Harris and got away with it.

The day before the fourteenth, I went over to Wendy's Place a little early to pick up Rachel. I figured we could go for a swim in the rec pool and then lie in the sun before going home for supper. Rach is a water bug; I taught her to swim myself when she was two. She practices diving while I swim laps, and won't come out till every inch of her round little body is blue going to purple.

Wendy's was closed and no one was there, so I headed for the park. It was a beautiful day, and I just assumed that's where everyone'd be. They weren't by the swings, so I headed out behind them, to the baseball field. From a distance I could see seven kids in a circle with two adults; Rach and Nicole were in the middle, dodging two big, light balls with great expertise, if I do say so myself. I hadn't realized Wendy had hired another assistant, so I was surprised to see the second adult. As I got closer, I realized it was a man, but before I could think more about it, Rach came racing toward me and swooped up into my arms.

"Hi, mom. I've been in the middle for hours and no one can hit me, not even Mac."

"Who's Mac?"

"Oh, he's a friend. He plays ball with us almost every day now."

I made a mental note to ask Wendy who he was, and pantomimed swimming so she'd know where we were going, and then Rach and I were off.

McQUADE
13.

I GREW REALLY FOND OF THAT KID, BUT I knew if I kept seeing her I'd get no further than square two. Although I hoped to God I wasn't at square one. I still wasn't sure. The mother hadn't done anything extraordinary since I had discovered her, except raise a terrific kid, study a lot, and dance until she had to be exhausted. None of that seemed like the activities of a first-class thief. And because I liked her kid as much as I did, I knew I was getting more and more prone to drop the whole thing, sail down to Mexico, and when I got back in a month or so, hotfoot it over the bridge and try to make time with her. The idea wouldn't let go; it was infinitely more appealing than the reformation route. Of course, if I succeeded, it might get serious because of the little girl. I'm not much of a moralist, but you can't mess around with a lady who owns a pretty nice and happy child. The mother could get miserable, and that would affect the kid. Then too, I had to protect her in case McCraken got wise and started to hit the colleges.

What was happening to thick-skinned McQuade and lady-killer McQuade and the newest hotshot detective in town? He was turning into a nauseating knight McQuade. I had to get away from both the kid and the mother; I was becoming someone I didn't know at all.

I decided to try a new tack to get to know what made the lady tick. I dressed in some casual slacks, resurrected an old pipe I hadn't smoked since Yale, threw on an old, worn but attractive plaid shirt, and headed for Dwinelle. My name was Max Roberts, and I was disguised as a roving reporter for the *San Francisco Chronicle*, doing a story on "The Life of the Graduate Student."

I two-stepped up the stone stairs and made the first right I came to. Out came the pipe, and then I hit the steps going down to the basement. At the bottom, I meandered down the hall, praying I'd run into one of the weirdos who cohabited with Tony in what was euphemistically called an office. No one was wandering around in the hall, but I heard voices coming out of the room. One of them was Tony's. I made it to the men's room in half a second and leaned up against the wall, panting like a crazy man. What the hell was she doing there. She was supposed to be over at Bancroft, teaching those little kids how to inhale and exhale. I strained at the door and was sure I heard a very light tread go down the hall and up the steps. I peeped out a couple of minutes later. Silence. I snuck by the room again and was just past when I felt a woman's hand on my shoulder.

"Can I help you?" a voice whined up at me from behind a pair of tinted specs. My stomach unknotted; it was the woman who shared Tony's office.

"Yeah. Maybe you can." I held out a paw. "The name's Max Roberts. I'm a reporter on the *Chronicle*, doing a story about the life of the graduate student, and I'm looking for some people to interview." I looked questioningly down at her and smiled.

A slow pink crawled up her neck and landed on her cheeks, spotting them with pink, rather than covering them, and giving her a rather sick and mottled look.

"Why, yes, I think I could. I think I could spare the time."

She stuck her head in the room. "Tom, I'm going over to the Terrace. Be back in half an hour, okay?"

All I heard in reply was a mumbled male grumble. It sounded like "sure honey."

She babbled all the way over to the cafeteria. By the time we got there I was beginning to think I should have gone to the park with Rachel. I had no idea what the hell to ask the woman or what it was I was even after. She was such a big talker, it turned out not to be much of a problem. Apparently Tom, her husband, and another fellow, named Dick, were the only ones actually doing any thesis writing. The others were still at various stages of course work, going ahead at average speed.

"Except for Tony. She's taking so many courses this summer that she'll be able to start doing her research by the spring." She tried to look playful, though God only knows why. "And she started a whole year after me."

That seemed like a pretty good opening; at least we could discuss Tony.

"Is she in some sort of a hurry or something?" I queried, all innocence.

"Well, yes. She has a four-year-old daughter and no husband, so she needs to get through as quickly as possible."

"I don't mean to be obtuse, but why does having a child mean she has to speed up the graduate-school process?"

"Have you ever been a graduate student?"

I shook my head no. "Coffee or tea?"

"Tea. Coffee makes me nervous."

Obviously she had been drinking a lot of it. Her giggle was driving me up a wall. Nevertheless, I found myself asking, "What difference does it make?"

"Because then you'd know how broke we all are."

She seemed to be winding up for more babble, so I broke in with a question.

"What do you all do for money?"

"Well, Teddy's wife works in an office and I've got Tom. Dick grumbles a lot."

"And Tony?"

"I don't know. She teaches dance to little girls, which can't bring in a lot. She did have a guy in the poli sci department, but I think that's over now."

"She shouldn't have dumped him till she finished

school," I tried to grin conspiratorially. Maybe the reporter gimmick would pay off after all.

"She didn't. Christopher dumped her. He didn't like the way she was or something like that. I don't understand Tony too well sometimes. Hey, this doesn't have anything to do with anything."

"Sorry," I commiserated. "I didn't mean to go off base."

I didn't want her suspicions aroused, so I settled in to asking her all the questions she expected to get: what kinds of courses she was taking, which she liked and which she didn't, what kind of research she did and what it entailed. I had to sit there and pretend interest for over an hour. Which was pretty hard, considering her whine and that I had already gotten what I had come for.

I kept wondering what the political scientist hadn't liked about the way Tony was.

On the way back across campus, Leslie suggested I talk to her husband, Tom. That way I'd get "a totally unbiased view of graduate-student life—half female and half male." I bowed out, explaining that I'd already interviewed three male students, one in chemistry, one in English, and one in law. Another interview with a woman had already been set up for me in the political science department by the *Chronicle*, and I was already late. I ran off before she could protest.

Of course, my mind was on a Christopher in the political science department, and as I raced through the front doors of Barrows Hall, my eyes were already searching the directory in search of a professor with the right first name. There were two. The first one passed me as he headed for the men's room; he was gray and in his fifties and didn't look like Tony's type. The other had an office in the basement, which indicated his status and, presumably, his age. The door was closed so I knocked. He opened it himself, blue book in hand. His looks surprised me.

He was the type they call tall, dark, and handsome, and he reminded me of a pedantic Hunter. Hunter at least had a sense of humor. I put a reign on my mind and tried to give him the benefit of the doubt. Perhaps he was preoccupied with the tests he was grading. Still, I couldn't help but think that he was the first aspect of the lady's life that rang a little bit sour.

I held out my hand and introduced myself. "Hi. The name's Max Roberts. I'm a reporter on the *Chronicle*, doing a story on the life of the female graduate student. I think I'll be concentrating on a girl named Antonia Weiner. I'm told you know her pretty well."

He took on a very strained look. "Hello. Christopher Tanner. Excuse me." He set his book down and sat in a big swivel desk chair.

"Tony and I are no longer seeing each other, so I don't think I'll be much help."

"Anything you might know about her that her fellow graduate students wouldn't, would be a help." I tried a serious demeanor.

He visibly blanched and attempted to smile. His face looked contorted.

"You really mean anything?"

"Hey, man. I'm not writing a pornographic novel, just an article."

"That's not what I had in mind either. Oh, never mind." He swiveled to his desk and back. He seemed like a very uptight fellow. He asked me, "What do you want to know?"

But didn't let me tell him. He went on all by himself.

"She's bright and beautiful and warm and loving, and she works hard as hell to make ends meet."

"Come on. That's what everyone says, but she can't be perfect. Why'd you break up?"

"I don't believe that's any of your business."

"Sorry. No offense meant."

Neither of us spoke, but the man clearly did not enjoy being a prig.

"It was a personality clash, as they say. We're trying to be friends."

"I'm sorry."

"Yes. Well, I've got work to do and I don't really have anything else to say."

I left without another word, except thanks, wondering all the way back to Dwinelle what the personality clash had been about. I ran into Tony headed out Sather Gate. There was quite a crowd scurrying from one class to another, so she didn't seem to notice me. I picked up the tail. Since I had lost track of her the last couple of days, what with my other activities, I figured it was a good idea.

She headed across University Avenue and turned up Durant. I was positive she was on her way to Wendy's Place. She was taking my favorite route, and she was walking. It took a little over half an hour to get there—she stopped at Bud's for an ice cream cone and nibbled at it as she walked. We got to Wendy's at a little after three. I waited outside about halfway down the block. The lady came out in about fifteen minutes without the kid. She had evidently dumped an overstuffed shopping bag she had been carrying, because she was empty-handed. This was not the usual routine.

I followed her up the block. I had trouble keeping up because I was a little short of breath, but I held my tail. Then I almost lost her at the Co-op when she bummed a ride in the parking lot. I put my thumb out, told the girl who stopped I was a private eye—like Jim Rockford but I lived on a boat—and that I was following someone. She had never heard of Rockford but pulled out neat and pretty just the same. We stayed on College Avenue and didn't turn until we were past the Café Romano. I had her stop and let me off because I knew where we were headed by then. Back to home base.

I stood outside, up the block, and waited. After about half an hour I sat down on the curb. Maybe she was staying in to study. I was just about to give up and go get some coffee to go, when she came prancing out the front door. I held my breath but felt it whistle out just the same. She had on an old, supertight pair of jeans and a blazing blue leotard. The same outfit she wore to rip off Hunter. My stomach slid down to my toes; I closed my eyes for a couple of seconds and took stock. Of what? Her life? My life? Shit. When I opened them, all I could see was the blue of her leotard as she headed up the block. The pieces fell into place of their own accord; I couldn't help but get the picture. The "personality clash" had been over the girl's sideline. Mr. Uptight could never accept his girl being a cat burglar. Hell, who could?

I almost missed the bus because my mind had been working overtime and I had fallen a full block behind her. I caught it, hopped on, and slid into a seat a couple of rows behind, but she had spotted me and I had rung some kind of bell in her head, because she turned around and stared. I did the obvious, winking and grinning my most leering grin, until the little head spun right back around and the muscles across the blue back tightened under the thin fabric. Her head stayed rigidly front for the whole ride and she never once looked back, not even when she got off on the other side of the bay.

She caught a second bus on Market Street and I caught the very next one. I was being cautious, because I couldn't take the chance of her spotting me again. Lucky for me, the traffic was pretty thick, so the buses stayed back to back and I saw her jump off at Montgomery. Instead of taking the trolley up and over, she started to hike, turning her head around to search the streets every couple of feet. I stayed way back, making sure some big lug was always in front of me. As far as I know, she never spotted my tail.

She was almost at the crest of the hill when she turned a corner. As she did, she looked over her shoulder. I ducked into a vestibule and stayed put a couple of seconds. No one showed, so I started moving. By the time I got to the corner, I was sure I had lost her. There was no one in sight, but out of the corner of my eye I saw a flash of blue ducking into what appeared to be a vacant lot a third of the way down the block. I picked up speed, wanting to run to the spot, but held back because of the sound my shoes made on the pavement. I didn't have on sneakers; they didn't go with my reporter role. I was almost on top of it before I realized where she had gone. A few feet in front of me was the entranceway to one of those small green alleys that pass for courtyards all through the Knob Hill area of San Francisco. I tried to peer in as cautiously as possible, but my location was poor. If she had been in front of the first house down the alley and turned her head even slightly, she would have spotted me, full face. Luckily, her back was toward me and she was bending down over what looked to be a medium-sized suitcase. Where the hell had that come from? I slipped out of my loafers and made my way up the steps of the building that fronted the alley. Underneath, maybe. The steps were cold as hell, but it was better than chancing her hearing me climbing up. I stood up against the door, as flat as I could, and turned my head. I had a view of about half the alley. She was three houses down, unloading her rope.

With almost breathtaking ease she looped one end around her butt, holding the rest like some sort of lasso. In what appeared to be slow motion she started swinging the thing around and around her head. The whirling rope, which seemed to have some sort of hook attached to the other end, hit the roof ledge, vibrated, and stuck firm. She had done it with only one throw. Tugging and pulling, she didn't move until she was sure it was firm.

In one sure, catlike movement she jumped up, her back arched down to the ground, and planted her feet firmly against the building. Her curled-up body was only several feet from the earth below, in a position parallel to it. Slowly, she started to climb up the building, using the rope for leverage and her feet for traction.

About halfway up the building she stopped and stretched her body out until she was one solid line parallel to the ground. Slowly, the arm gripping the rope stretched up and out till it was above and behind her. Then she arched her back, belly out, and hung there, while she rubbed the small of her back with the other hand. It was a beautiful and incredible stunt, and it was over almost before it had begun. Seconds later, she paused at a tiny window, pulled it open, and slid in. First went the head, then the tummy, next the round and luscious-looking behind, and last the feet dipped up and were gone. She left the rope hanging, so I stayed put. I assumed she would come down the same way she had gone up, and I was right.

She spent only about half an hour in the house, at the most. About five minutes after she had disappeared, a young couple made their way down the alley and into a house beyond my scope of vision. They were too engrossed in each other to notice the dangling rope, but I didn't let out my breath until I heard the slam of the door as it shut behind them. What a chance she had taken! She couldn't possibly control the movements of every person who lived on that tiny alley. She had to choose a time and do her thing. If someone appeared—curtains. The girl had chosen a good time to slip into the brownstone: 7:15. Right after people get home from work, and before they go out for the evening.

Her head appeared at the window at about 7:40, then ducked back inside. She came out feet first, crouched half in and half out of the window, then grasped the rope with her right hand and swung on. Her legs wrapped around the rope and she slid down, fireman-style. I didn't wait to see how she landed, although I was tempted, but got the hell away. For the first time in months I wanted a martini. Extradry.

14.

I KNEW SOMETHING WAS WRONG THE MINUTE
I got on the bus. The driver was about to pull away from
the curb when this medium-sized, muscular blond guy
started to pound on the doors. The bus stopped and he
got on, choosing a seat a few behind mine. Problem was,
he looked familiar. I turned around to get a better look,
and the face tried to leer at me in a suggestive way; he
was quite unsuccessful. Still, I felt myself beginning to
blush like an idiot, so I turned right back around again.
The whole way into the city I kept trying to place the
face, but I just couldn't. He wasn't the guy from the
ice cream parlor, but I knew that I did know him

from someplace. The premonition was there, in the chestbone right above my breasts, that something was wrong. Very wrong, and the guy set it off.

When we stopped at the terminal, I got off the bus as fast as I could and jumped right on another at Market Street. He didn't follow. Even after I got off at Montgomery, my head kept swiveling around to survey the crowd, just in case. About three blocks from the top of the hill, I thought I saw someone duck into a vestibule, but after staring as hard as I could I chalked it up to "Tony's paranoia" and continued hiking. Probably someone scurrying along, in a rush to get home. I picked up my own pace and turned into Harris's alley. I bent down and looked under the staircase of the house that fronted the alley, and, sure enough, there sat my little trusty suitcase right where I had stashed it the day before, filled with rope and squished-in mountain-climbing shoes. I lugged it to the little back courtyard of Harris's house. Before opening it, I ran back to the tip of the alley and looked around. Again I was sure I saw a flash a few doors down, but it was nothing definite, merely enough to increase the pounding in my upper chest. Had I the time, I would have tried some yoga to loosen up. As it was, I raced back to the suitcase, unloaded as quick as I could, switched shoes, stuffing my ballet slippers into the back pocket of my jeans, quickly looping the rope around my butt. The muscles across the back of my neck and shoulders were stiff as hell, so I did a couple of rag dolls before the first throw. Much to my amazement the hook caught the first time around. Considering how stiff my arm was, and my intense anxiety about something being wrong, it was pretty amazing.

Hanging onto the rope as tight as I could with both arms, I swung my feet up and began to climb. The houses on either side of the Harris place were dark, but the one at the end of the alley on the right had a couple of lights on. I wanted to get up to the window and in before anyone decided to go out to dinner. It took no more than three or four minutes. I tried to pull up the window with my left hand, but it felt stuck. I gave it one more try, and up it went. I was inside in seconds and lucky as hell. Moments later a young lovesick couple came sauntering up the alley. My breath caught, and stayed held, until they passed the rope that was still swinging back and forth outside the window. Luckily it was already getting dark, and you couldn't see much anyway unless you were looking for something. Which they obviously weren't, other than each other.

It was a good hit. The guy had a couple of beautiful little ashtrays around, Wedgewood written all over the bottom, a lovely antique silver necklace and matching bracelet that even looked like it might have been made in Berkeley (for some lucky lady who would now never receive it), and spare change amounting to a little under a thousand dollars in cash. Can you imagine leaving that kind of bread lying around your bedroom? Can you imagine having that kind of bread to leave lying around!

This guy was even crasser than any of the others had been. He didn't have his money stashed in a sock or a pretty little silver box or a gold cup. His was stuffed into an overflowing little basket, probably purchased at Pier One. The bills—mostly twenties—hung out all over the left-hand side of his dresser top. When I had stuffed them into my bag, the dresser looked surprisingly barren. I figured money alone would carry me through the following spring, and by then I'd be able to pick up a couple of courses to teach at Berkeley extension. Warren was already yammering away about the possibility, so I knew it wasn't one of my fanciful pipe dreams. What the hell! I could close off my mind and rattle off the dissertation. Then I'd open it all back up and become a terrific teacher, like Christopher. Maybe this was really the last job, and that's what the pounding in the chest had been all about. I got out of there quick, not even bothering to check out the kitchen or the living room. I had enough; why be greedy?

Going down, I had a bit of trouble closing the window. Somehow it seemed harder to balance myself knowing I had all that distance still to go, than to do it when the trip was almost over. Still, I got it closed in seconds and slid down the rope fireman-style, with very little difficulty. For some reason, when I hit bottom, I really hit. I must have misjudged the distance or something, because I really scraped up one of my knees. I could feel it bleeding right through my dungarees. The stuff was slung over my shoulder in the canvas bag, and I was schlepping the suitcase, switching it from hand to hand. About halfway down the hill, I decided lugging the rope all the way back to Berkeley was ridiculous. I knew Rachel and I would survive for a long time to come on what I picked up that evening, so why should I take unnecessary chances? I sat down in a vestibule and unloaded the rope. I found an empty garbage can a third of the way down a side street and dumped it in. I went back for the suitcase, took another street, found another can and dumped it in as well. I tied the shoes together and slung them over my back. You could never tell who I'd take up with next. If he was an outdoors type, I might need mountain-climbing shoes.

Rachel was exhausted when I picked her up at Wendy's house. The commune had found a stray dog and he had apparently been running Rach ragged. I was relieved; at least someone could tire her out and she wasn't invincible. I picked her up in my arms, cradling her there, and carried her to the bus stop. It was amazing, but after the suitcase she seemed light as a feather. She went right to bed, no bath, no story, and was asleep before her head nestled into her pillow. I had a huge dish of ice cream and two glasses of wine before turning in, and slept like a log.

ANTONIA
15.

I WAS AWAKE BY SIX THE FOLLOWING morning. Something really was wrong, and I knew it. The guy on the bus was somebody I had seen before; the vestibule runner wasn't a figment of my imagination. I was in danger; and if I was, so was my kid. Should I move, leaving no forwarding address behind to incriminate me? If I did, could I write the dissertation from some outside place and send it in to Warren when I was finished? I lay there for almost an hour trying to decide what to do. Was it bad enough for me to leave Berkeley? If I decided to leave I could always tell Warren my mother was sick and I had to take care of her.

No, he was too big a busybody and would call Short Hills
moments after I left, to make sure everything was okay.
Any ounce of reason I possessed had fled with the coming of dawn, and terror had taken over. When Rachel
got up, she stood in the doorway staring at me for a
good five seconds before I even noticed her. Usually I
hear her stirring and call her in to bed with me, so this
was a real and obvious change.

"Are you okay, Mommy?" a nervous little voice inquired.

"Sure I am. Aren't you coming into bed?" I tried to
force cheer into my voice.

"You don't seem okay. Want me to rub your back?"

"Um h'mm. That would be lovely."

She sat on me, and moved her hands around in what
passed for rubbing, and jumped up and down a few
times "riding the horse," a game she has played since
she was old enough to sit up and get on top of me. After
a few minutes of that, she tumbled off, falling on her
side and giggling, giggling, giggling. She kissed me on
the neck and cheek and mouth, then sat bolt upright.

"Do you feel better now?"

"A little bit, honey."

With that she got on to ride again, tickling me at the
same time. Since I am horribly ticklish and always have
been, she had me laughing in seconds. As soon as I was
really going at it, she jumped off the bed and told me to
get dressed so we could go to Wendy's.

"What's the big rush?"

"We're going to the park this morning. Mac's going to
teach us how to play baseball!"

Everything went gray, then black. That was it—the blond guy on the bus, trying to look hip but not quite making it. He was the same one I had seen playing dodge ball in the park. I had sworn I would ask Wendy about him, but I had been very busy plotting out the Harris thing, so I had forgotten. The bottom left my stomach, the world caved in, and I wanted to die. What was this guy doing in my life? Why was he playing with my kid? What the hell had he been doing on that bus? And—oh, shit, had he been the shadow I thought I saw ducking into the vestibule as I hiked up California the night before?

"Mommy, what's wrong?"

Rachel was on top of me again, kissing me and hugging and looking the way she looked. I pretended a calm I feared I'd never feel again, rolled over, held her tightly around her middle, and asked, "Honey, where'd you meet Mac?"

"Outside of Bancroft."

I was trying to hold on with all I was worth.

"Bancroft? What was he doing there?"

"Going to a class. He caught my ball and threw it back to me."

"And? . . ."

"And then he started coming to play with me every day, and then I asked him to come to the park and he said yes. You should meet him, Mommy. I know he'd make you feel better."

I didn't even answer her, just kept on grilling.

"What does he do, Rachel?"

"He studies something."

"What?"

"I don't know, Mommy; what's wrong?"

"Nothing. What else does he do?"

"He worked someplace, but he quit."

She paused to look at me, but my face must have scared her into trying to remember more.

"He works on his boat."

"What boat, honey?"

"His boat. The one he lives on."

I pounced. "Where? Do you know where?"

"I think he said in Sausalito."

"Are you sure, honey. Try to remember."

Rachel was biting her lip, and I wanted to hug her but I was too scared. She was going to cry, but she held back and shook her head yes.

I scooped her up on my way to the phone.

"What time do you go to the park?"

"Lunchtime."

I knew I couldn't live with the fear of who he was and what he wanted hanging over me until then. If we hurried, we might be able to catch him before he left his boat.

"Hi, Wendy? Tony. Listen, Rachel won't be coming in today. No, nothing's wrong. I don't have any classes, so I thought we'd take the day to be together, maybe take the ferry across the bay. Thanks, I'm sure we will."

Rachel didn't say a word; she just hung onto my neck and watched me. She, too, knew that something was up. I dialed again.

"Extension 1838, please. Yes, I'll hold . . . ."

"Who're you calling, Mommy?"

"Professor Warren."

She hugged me tighter.

"Hi, Madeline. Did Warren get in yet? . . . Yeah, thanks. . . . Hi, Professor. Do you mind if I bring back those *Pravda*s tomorrow? . . . Well, it's such a beautiful day, and Rach has been begging me all morning to take her on a boat ride, and since I only have to come to campus to drop off those papers . . . You're a doll; thanks a lot. See you tomorrow. . . . We will, thanks to you."

I hung up and set Rachel down all in one movement. The condition of Rachel's bureau drawers was impossible, so it took several minutes for me to find the pastel-striped pinafore my mother had sent her in the beginning of the summer. She looks like an angel in it, and that is what I wanted. She squirmed around at first when I tried to pull the dress down over her head, but the look on my face told her it wasn't such a hot idea, and she became still.

"I can put on my shoes, Mommy. You go get dressed."

I chose my one Marimekko dress. It's a splash of blues and purples and greens, cut way back off the shoulder blades in front and scooped out in a V in back. It sashes at the waist with a very thick waistband and makes me look slim and tall and youthful. I brushed my hair at least a thousand strokes, so it looked soft and full and hung just right down my back. I pulled out a navy canvas bag I hadn't bothered switching to for the summer and stuffed my wallet and comb and junk into it as fast as I could. Rachel had finished with her shoes and was watching me from the hallway.

"What's wrong, Mommy?"

"Nothing, honey."

"Then why are we getting dressed up?"

I sat her down next to me on the bed and tried to be a calm, thoughtful mother. My stomach was doing cartwheels, and I knew my eyes weren't focusing quite right, but I tried.

"I really do want to spend the day with you, Rach. I thought we'd go into San Francisco and have some ice cream at Ghirardelli Square, and take the ferry to Sausalito, and, if we have time, look for your friend, Mac."

"Can I have a hot fudge sundae?"

"Um h'mm." She still looked skeptical, but the sundae won out over the uncertainty. Maybe she figured I had my period. She had learned all about it at Wendy's a few weeks before and had been fascinated. Apparently some other kid had asked what it was, so Wendy dug out a very funny book, and the kids all read it together. Anyhow, suddenly she was raring to go.

"Come on, Mommy. Let's go. We'll miss the bus and have to wait for hours."

"Just let me brush my teeth, honey, and then we'll go."

"You already did that."

"Well, I want to do it again."

"Hurry up, Mommy! Come on!"

She grabbed me before I had a chance to pick up my brush and give my hair a few more strokes, and then we were out the door and down the steps. She wouldn't let me take the stroller, informing me she was too old for it and that she could walk. We ran the last few feet to the bus and just caught it as it was pulling off. We switched buses to go across the bay; there were no seats—rush hour—so I had to hold Rachel in my arms.

The second we got off the bus, she informed me, "I'm starved, Mommy."

Even in my nervous state I couldn't keep from smiling. I grabbed her hand and we ran for the trolley at Market and Hyde.

"Then come on!"

The conductor kept her pretty busy, so I was free to concentrate. Only I couldn't. I knew I had to find "Mac," and ask him directly what he wanted from me, or I'd go nuts. But I didn't have the faintest idea how I was going to do it. What would I do—act cool and offer him half of what I had gotten? Or did I beg him not to turn me in, pointing out that he would be ruining two lives, not just one? No, that wouldn't work. I'd offer myself to him for the day, or night, or whatever it took. The idea was sickening, truly sickening, but it was less nauseating than being stuck at Santa Rita with Rachel God-knows-where. The more I tried to figure out a course of action, the more terrified and illogical I became. By the time the trolley got to the last stop, I wasn't making any sense at all, even to myself.

Rach tugged and pulled at me and pointed to the square and started to run across the street, paying no attention whatsoever to cars or people or buses. That knocked me back to earth and I grabbed her up into my arms to protect her and hug her and hold her close to me.

"Rachel! I told you never to run into the street like that. Look at all the cars!"

"I'm sorry, Mommy"—and then I got a kiss and then she was squirming in my arms so she could see the ice cream place as soon as it came into sight. She got her sundae and made me have some, too—"At least get one scoop of coffee, Mommy"—and she took forever to finish. I tried to join her chatter, and to enjoy her enjoyment, but failed miserably. My mind was in Sausalito.

The ferry was late, so it took over an hour to get there. It was a horrid trip. Rachel raced all over the boat, tried to climb on the railing twice, almost fell overboard once, and was so excited she made an awful nuisance of herself. I was so anxious and upset by this time, I couldn't control her very well. When we were halfway across the bay I totally lost my cool and stood in the middle of the deck screaming at her like some awful version of "mother shrew." She started crying, and then I started crying, and we both made quite a sight. I was mortified.

The boat docked and Rachel wanted a hot dog. I gave in, partly to appease her and partly because I didn't want all my fellow passengers to think I was a totally horrendous mother. After all, I had been awful to her from the time we had gotten on the boat, and none of it had really been her fault. She ate her hot dog in big gulps and then asked for some fries. By this time I had gotten out my Maalox. She finished the fries, consumed an enormous float, and then was satisfied.

"Can we go find Mac, Mommy? Can we, can we?"

"Sure, honey, why not?"

Why not, indeed! I asked some girl in a halter and very short shorts where the boat basin was, and where boats with people living in them were, in particular, and she pointed the way. She didn't sound very sure of herself, so I asked a rather grizzled-looking old man as well. He pointed in a slightly different direction, so I didn't know what to do. Rach ran ahead, yelling, "Let's just walk till we find them. He'll be there, Mommy. I know he will."

We did find some boats in a few minutes, but none of them seemed to have any people living on them. There wasn't a soul in sight. We continued in the same direction for what felt like hours but didn't see anyone. Then I thought I saw a bobbing white cap on a boat a short way off, so we walked toward it. By this time, Rach had climbed from my arms to my shoulders for a piggyback ride, and I was exhausted, fighting to stay on top of all I was feeling.

"Hello." The white cap kept bobbing; he hadn't heard me, so I tried again. The second time I called out, he looked up.

"Can you tell me where the houseboats are, or the sailboats, the ones people live on?"

"You're at the wrong end of the marina for either one, lady. The folks that live on them big ugly houseboats tie 'em up past pier 20, all the way back that way. The sailboats have a couple of piers 'bout half a mile further on."

I wanted to die, and then something snapped. I took Rachel by the shoulder and gave her a shake. "Which one does he live on, Rach? Which one?"

She looked terrified; I had never shaken her before. I knew I had to pull myself together, so I let go, gently pinching her cheek.

"He said he wanted to take a trip on his boat . . ." She looked up at me hesitantly.

"Then it must be a sailboat," I assured us both.

I turned back and stood there dumbly staring at the old guy. I wasn't sure I remembered exactly what he had said. I cleared my throat. "Did you say half a mile past pier 20?"

"That's what I said, lady."

He went back to work. Rach ran in front of me, yelling back, "I can walk all the way. You won't have to carry me. Come on, Mommy. You'll be so glad when you meet him. He's nice; I know you'll like him. He's much nicer than Christopher."

Great! Maybe he'd want to support me, and marry me, and live with me happily ever after. . . .

We walked and walked and walked for almost an hour, alternating between Rachel running ahead and picking up little rocks to hurl in the water, and me carrying her up on my shoulders the way Michael used to when she was a little baby. God, I hadn't thought about Michael in months. I wondered what he'd think if he saw me now. Rachel kept apologizing every time she got too tired to walk, but I was too terrified to reassure her much. I wanted a clearer picture of the boat so I would know for sure when I spotted it.

"Rachel, honey. Do you know what color Mac's boat is?"

"White . . . with something blue . . ."

Marvelous. I tried to keep the rising hysteria out of my voice.

"A blue sail? Or blue sides with a white sail?"

"It has a lady's name." She smiled up at me, delighted to have thought of it.

"That's all you remember, honey?"

"I think it's painted on the side, Mommy . . ."

She looked very worried, so I picked her up and hugged her to me.

"It's okay, Rachie. We'll find it."

Moments later we passed the houseboats, low-slung little things, riding heavily in the water, squat and square and not nearly as sleek as the boat the man who gave me directions had been working on.

"We're there, Mommy!" Rachel squirmed to the ground and ran up ahead.

"Almost," I answered, barely fighting back the desire to turn and run all the way back to Berkeley. And indeed, soon we reached the sailboats: some obviously expensive, with sails, and gear, and all the stuff you must need if you're going to go around the world in a boat; and then the smaller variety, older, for boat enthusiasts. There was a skinny girl with no boobs, working at scrubbing the deck of a fairly modest but pretty ketch about fifty feet ahead of us. I looked at my watch and was most surprised to find it was only 10:15. We had left the house at seven thirty. I was sure it was past twelve. I called out hello when we were about fifteen feet from her boat. The girl heard us coming and looked up.

"Hi. What can I do for you?"

I set Rachel down and took her hand. "We're looking

for a guy who lives on a boat out here, and I thought maybe you could help us."

"I can try. What's his name?"

"Mac," Rachel's voice sang out. "He's big and blond and really nice."

"He is, is he?" The girl laughed. "You sure have come to the right place. He lives next door. I think you're a little early, though. Mac went on a real bender last night and didn't get home till dawn. He's probably dead to the world."

My heart was beating like mad and I could feel the color draining out of my face. I looked at the white sailboat in the next slip. "How do we get on board?"

"Just climb over the edge—pull the boat toward you if you can't make that step—and then ring the cowbell hanging over the bright blue hatch."

"I told you it was white and blue," Rachel squeaked with delight. "Come on!"

I patted her head, bewildered by her mood; I could hardly breathe. I said thanks to the girl. I made Rachel stand behind me while I leaned over and tugged at the boat. It moved in the water and we climbed on, Rachel riding my back. I set her down immediately and tried to catch my breath.

"Come on, Mommy. Ring the bell!"

Rachel had started jumping up and down in her excitement.

Not knowing what else to do, I rang it. And then I rang it again, but no one came. By this time my throat was parched from anxiety. I gave it one last try.

"He must have left already, honey. Maybe we'll catch him when he comes home." I took Rachel's hand and turned to go. I didn't know whether to be relieved or upset, and hadn't even decided when I felt her tugging at me. My eyes followed her around and I tried fruitlessly to swallow. The hatch slid back and the shutters swung open.

It was him. Disheveled, with a pair of ragged cutoffs hastily pulled over his hips, chest tan, eyes half awake. Rachel practically jumped into his arms.

"Mac! Mac! We're here. We took the ferry and then I got my mommy to help me find you."

He held her and gave her a kiss but never took his eyes from my face.

"Hello, Tony."

"Hello, Mac."

I was fighting to keep back the tears and he knew it. I could have kicked myself; I wanted so to be cool and on top of the situation—in charge. But I wasn't. I was still me.

The man lifted my child way above his head and spun her around up there, and she was, of course, delighted.

"You want to see the boat, kid?"

"Oh, yes, Mac, yes," she squealed, never giving me a second glance. They seemed so utterly natural together. I thought of Michael and all Rachel was missing and found myself even closer to tears. Numbly, I followed the two of them down the five narrow steps leading to wherever. I guess to where he lived. My eyes were misting, and I was trying like hell to control it. What did he want with me? No matter how hard I tried to figure it out, I couldn't get anywhere. The effort was driving me crazy; it was all so absurd, incomprehensible.

His boat was nice: first came what looked like a little

pullman kitchen, with the stove and sink to the left, up against the wall of the boat; and a counter top with spices running along a shelf above it on the right; with the refrigerator underneath. I figured the top lifted up. The area beyond was fixed up like a living room/dining room combination. Two foam-and-wood sofas (berths, I guess) faced each other across a pull-out butcher block table. One glass stood in the middle, and an empty bottle of Scotch. The sofas were covered with fluffy pillows in bright primary colors. Even so, the rya rug under the table was startling.

In the hall beyond was a closed door—bathroom, I guessed—and a big, firm-looking double bed, high up. An overstuffed chair butted up against the door.

Suddenly, I didn't feel Rachel's little body at my back and turned around to find her. She was crawling around in a tight little area beyond the stairs where a little hammock was rigged up. The man said something about the former tenants preparing for a baby, but I didn't pay much attention. I was too nervous.

"Oh, Mac, it's just perfect. Whoever slept here would just have to remember not to jump out of bed in the morning and then they wouldn't hit their head." Rachel was in seventh heaven.

"Would you like to sleep there, Rachel?" His eyes were gentle as he asked, and I couldn't stand it.

"She has a place to sleep!" I glared at him.

"For the time being." He looked right into my eyes.

"Forever." Oh, please, mister. Please don't turn me in. I'm a mommy first and foremost. Everything else has been a horrible aberration.

But he couldn't hear. The grin spreading across his face was particularly frightening. "Why? Are you planning to live in Berkeley until you're old and gray?"

I couldn't smile. My throat was too dry. "I haven't planned that far ahead."

His gray green eyes seemed to be taking me apart while he watched me speak. As he made his way back to the galley, he asked if either of us wanted anything to drink.

"I make great coffee, ladies."

"I'd like some milk, please."

"Rachel!"

Then the bell attached to the blue hatch jangled. I almost jumped out of my skin.

"I'll get it." Rachel skipped over to the steps, happy to be meeting a friend of Mac's, but it was unnecessary. A rough Irish voice helloed, and a pair of legs in navy pants appeared in the hatchway.

"Hey, Mac, you there?"

When Mac turned to greet his visitor, the expression on his face was peculiar; but I didn't know him well enough to judge what it meant, which made me all the more nervous.

A beefy pink face topped with a minuscule streak of gray hair came level with Mac's and swiveled to take me in. "I can come back after I check out the new dance store in Mill Valley . . ."

Mac turned to me and smiled, but his face still looked peculiar. Why did he look so odd?

"That's okay, Crackin. This is Tony and her daughter, Rachel." He reached into the cabinet above the stove and came out with a glass jar stuffed with ginger po-gens, Rachel's favorite cookie. I was feeling so paranoid by this time that I even wondered if he had stocked up on them for this very occasion. He handed her two, with a large glass of foaming milk.

"Oh, boy, you remembered!" Rachel chirped, dancing over to give the man a quick hug and kiss. Jesus Christ! Who the hell was he? And who was the other man; and why was he checking out a dance store in Mill Valley. Oh, God.

I dumbly watched the blond man scoop my child up in his arms, bite her ear, and tell her she could go top-side if she wanted to.

"Just watch yourself, kid, and don't lean over the edge to look at the water. Can we trust you?"

"Oh, yes! You can trust me. Can't he, Mommy?" The eyes Rachel turned to me were filled to the brim with glee. I tried to speak but the sound that came out was so bizarre that I decided to smile instead, shaking my head yes at the same time. My grin looked similar to the one plastered across Mac's face.

"Great. Have a ball, kid." He set her down gently, gave her a pat on the behind, and sent her on her way. The other man stepped out of the way: before she dis-appeared through the hatch she turned to add, "He's much nicer than Christopher, Mommy!" and was gone. My head was spinning, and the "Rachel" I cried out in protest was feeble indeed. The beefy man smiled at me and shrugged—"That's kids for ya." I wanted to dig a hole and crawl into it.

Mac handed his friend a cup of coffee. "What's this

about a dance store? I thought you gave up on that case months ago." The peculiar look was back on his face.

"Thanks." Crackin's scarred pink fist closed around the coffee mug and he took a gulp of hot liquid. "The chief reopened it this morning."

Chief? Chief of what?

Mac held out another cup of coffee to me—"Cream or sugar?"

I just shook my head no, desperately fighting to hold back the tears. I could hear Rachel's little voice laughing above but couldn't make out her words. She must have been talking to the girl on the next boat. Suddenly, I wanted to hold her in my arms, kiss her cheek, taste her tears, soothe one of her colds.

Mac merely nodded and took a sip of the hot black liquid himself. "I haven't read the paper yet." His attention returned to the other man, who was leaning up against the refrigerator counter.

"Nothin' in it. Chief wants to keep it out of the news for a few days."

His eyes took me in, twinkling. "Remember the architect that was robbed over on Russian Hill a few months ago?"

I couldn't possibly have answered, so I shook my head no again.

"Never mind." He smiled and gestured with a thumb at Mac. "He can tell you about it sometime." His focus stayed there. "It looks like the girl in the blue leotard was the burglar after all. She pulled another job last night."

I started to cry.

The cop—because that's what he was, I realized, a cop—put down his mug and patted me on the head. "I'll talk to you some other time, Mac." He put his foot on the bottom step. Mac reached out and pulled me next to him, keeping a grip on my shoulder with his hand. I couldn't move and had to fight back the crazy urge to yell upstairs to Rach, "Get away!" I had to save her, but where could she go? I heard Mac's voice from miles away.

"Who saw her this time?"

"Some kid watching her big sister make out in the front vestibule." He had reached the top step, but Mac wasn't finished with him.

Of course he wasn't. His little burglar was right where he wanted her. He held on to me and asked, "Go on. Don't leave it there."

The cop chuckled. "You better watch that curiosity of yours. You never can tell where it'll lead ya!" But he seemed more than happy to explain. "The kid saw a pretty dark-haired little thing in faded jeans and a blue leotard bending over a suitcase in the alley, stuffing rope, or something—she isn't sure—inside. She didn't tell anyone about it until this morning, because she didn't want her big sister to know she was snooping."

Mac still wasn't satisfied. "Didn't the guy she ripped off report it last night?"

"Nope. Poor SOB doesn't even know he's been robbed. He's out of town at an ARCO convention."

I tried to move away, but Mac just tightened his grip and actually laughed. "If he works for ARCO, he deserved to be ripped off."

"That's what the chief's afraid of. He wants to wrap the whole thing up before the little lady becomes a local heroine."

He moved down a step, his inquisitive brown eyes looking directly at me. "Don't worry, honey. It'll all turn out okay. Mac here's quite a guy." Then he left.

I wiped the tears from my face with the back of my hand and jerked away from Mac, standing with my hands clenched until I felt the boat bounce. The cop was gone. Then I whirled on him, pushing out the words, "Who the hell are you, and what do you want from me?"

Rachel's little voice sounded behind me. "Are you all right, Mommy?"

I hadn't even heard her come down the stairs. Before I could pull myself together, Mac handed my daughter a cookie and quietly asked her to play outside for a little while longer. "Your Mommy and I need to talk, sweetie pie." The words sounded so reassuring. She nodded and slowly walked back up the steps, turning once to search our faces. I mouthed the words "I love you," and she disappeared. It seemed like she had come and gone before I could even touch her.

Mac moved toward me; I backed into a berth and had to sit down. He peered down at me and said, "I'm a good friend of Jessup Hunter III."

"Oh, dear God!"

He reached into his pocket and held out a handkerchief for me. When I didn't take it, he bent down and wiped my cheeks. I was so numb I hadn't even known I was crying.

"Please. What do you want from me?"

He turned away and leaned against the opposite berth. "When Jess hired me last year, I wanted to find you and make you pay: that antique jade ring you swiped was a family heirloom; it meant a lot to both of us." He knelt down and opened a drawer under the bunk. Then he held out a box to me. Inside was a perfect replica of the lovely little ring I had stolen and kept all this time because I couldn't bear parting with it, except the stone was opal instead of jade.

"Besides, you made him feel like an ass," he added, in a kind of mumble.

"It wasn't hard!" I thrust the box back at him, suddenly feeling terribly frustrated. Who was this man to put me through all this?

He merely grinned. "Probably not."

"I can give back his ring, but I hocked everything else," I managed, thinking maybe then he'd let me go before he called the cop. He seemed really fond of Rachel; he had to be thinking a little about what'll happen to her.

"That would be a start."

My voice didn't even shake when I asked, "And then what?"

He was still leaning up against the bunk, his face on his fist, so I couldn't see his expression when he answered, "You give everything back to everyone you stole it from and we all live happily ever after."

My chest felt constricted, like I might start to cry again. "That's a great idea!" Rachel's footsteps on the deck above sounded like the tread of a giant.

"I've got an even better one." He turned and stared at

me, his gray green eyes penetrating through to my soul. "You could be saved by a knight in slightly tarnished armor."

I wanted to laugh, but he wasn't even smiling. I thought it was such a funny thing to say, but his face was immobile; only his eyes moved over me from tip to toe. Then I caught on, my blood beginning to boil. His gentle demeanor was a good act; he was no different than any other stud.

"Jesus Christ!" I stood up and began to unbutton my dress, too angry even to feel disgusted with what was happening. "If I satisfy, do you promise to give me half a day's head start with my child before calling the cop?" I was shaking with fury; I wanted to haul off and hit him and hit him and hit him until he went down.

He grabbed my wrist before I reached the second button, his breathing harsh and labored, which seemed perfectly natural. "Cut it out!"

"Why?" I dropped my hand to my hip and glared at him. "Isn't this what you had in mind!"

He let go, glaring right back. "Look, lady, my life is almost as upside down as yours. I'm taking this one step at a time, too."

"Look, mister," I tried to hold my ground, "just tell me what you want. I can't take any more of this." My knees gave way and I sat back down on the foam cushion.

He moved toward me, never taking his eyes from mine, and squatted at my feet.

"Tony, Tony . . . what can I say? It kind of goes back a long way and isn't very clear in my mind. I went to

Choate, then Yale; hell, I grew up in a three-piece suit. I believed in all the stuff they taught us—good and bad, right and wrong, making it to the top. Of course, I was more than halfway there to start out with." He smiled.

"So?" He was choosing a wonderful time to be long-winded. I went to Short Hills High, Antioch, and Berkeley. So what!

Mac picked a speck of dirt off the rya rug and slowly tilted his face back up at me. "I don't want you to get caught."

My heart wasn't beating, I know it wasn't. "You mean you're not going to call that cop?"

He shook his head no and moved up on the bunk next to me. "But it's only a matter of time before he catches on. He'll make the jump from girl-with-a-social-conscience to school, too."

"Is that how you found me?"

"Kind of."

His right hand was almost touching mine. He moved it closer. "At least he doesn't know about the *Winnie-the-Pooh* . . ."

Suddenly I felt terribly embarrassed that Mac knew about it. I wanted to make amends, apologize, take the past year back. "I shouldn't have taken it, but Pooh Bear is Rachel's favorite."

"I know. She told me."

"We were in a market last year. Rach wanted one of those big Hershey bars—you know, those huge thick ones. I normally don't let her eat candy because of all the sugar, but when the checkout lady looked at the food stamps in my hand and told her to put the candy back because her mommy couldn't afford it . . ."

He took my hand before I finished the thought.

"Why don't you kiss her?"

Simultaneously, we swiveled toward the quiet little voice and away from each other. Neither of us had heard Rachel come down the steps. She looked so vulnerable standing in the galley, with one ponytail askew from playing, that I reached out my arms to her without uttering a word about what she had said. But she stayed put, looking from Mac to me and back again. He patted the cushion next to him. She idled down the steps but remained standing a few feet from us; when she inched closer, he picked her up and set her down. Rachie peered around Mac, a million questions in her eyes, but neither of us said anything.

"Ladies." Mac looked at me and then at Rachel. "How much do you know about sailing?"

"We've never even been on a boat before." Rachel's eyes were wide, again following the course from Mac to me and back.

He put his left arm around her and pulled her closer to his side. "That's good. That'll make it even harder for you to resist my offer." Before either of us could ask him what he meant, he hurried on. "How'd you like to take a trip with me to Mexico? Don't worry about not knowing how to sail"—he paused, glancing at me—"I taught the kid here how to play catch, and she's a fast learner. We'll just assume it runs in the family."

"Oh, Mommy, please, could we?" Rach jumped off the berth in a flurry of arms and legs, so excited.

"Take it easy, honey," I answered, my eyes on Mac.

But she couldn't, throwing her arms around me and planting wet little kisses on my nose and totally blocking my view. "You can write your paper for Mr. Warren there. Mac and I can do all the work on the boat!"

"If you still want to write it," Mac added, managing to make contact again around my squirming child.

"I don't know . . ." I desperately neded someone to talk to, someone to tell me what to do. Rachel slid off my lap and Mac's arm immediately went around me, ever so softly.

I could almost picture the sail of the boat as it caught the wind and suddenly wanted to stay on that boat with Mac and Rachel more than anything in the world. I wanted the whole year to be done with, that phase of my life over, finished.

Mac leaned over and kissed the top of Rachel's head.

"So, what do you say?" He bent over and kissed the top of my head. I wanted to touch the spot.

"It beats every other offer I have pending . . ."

Rachel hopped from one foot to the other. "Does that mean yes?"

Mac and I stared at each other, appraising. Or I appraised and he caressed, with the warmest eyes I had ever seen.

"I guess so."

She whooped and shrieked and ran from the steps to the stove, to the refrigerator, and back again.

When Mac finally spoke, it was almost in a whisper. "I still think you should give the ring back."

I couldn't help it—all the tension kind of released itself—I started to laugh. Rachel's giggle immediately joined in, and I could see Mac's eyes begin to dance and then he laughed. And laughed and laughed and laughed.

"You can have this one instead." He handed me back the little jewelry box.

A lump was forming in my throat. "You're some kind of nut."

"Mommy!" Rachel's tone was shocked. "That isn't polite!"

Mac's arm was still around my shoulder. He touched my cheek with three of his fingers. "It takes one to know one . . ." Then he tilted up my chin and ever so lightly brushed my lips with his. When he pulled back, I said, "That armor doesn't seem very tarnished to me."

"Can we go back to Berkeley first, Mommy? I want to take my Pooh Bear."

Mac stood and scooped her up into his arms, all in one lithe move. "Sure, kid. I'll take you back on my motorcycle." There were more squeals of delight from my kid as they headed up the steps; then he ducked his face back down. "Anything in particular you'd like to take along?"

In some kind of trance, I answered, "Some shorts and tops and the alfalfa sprouts I have growing in the kitchen window." We both grinned, and I felt more at ease than I had in years. "The ring's in my top right-hand drawer, under my panties."

"I'll leave it with the head teller on my way back," he replied, and then, anticipating what I was about to say—"He'll be having lunch at Poole's." Then he added, "I better drop off next month's rent with your super so no one'll come snooping. You can send any necessary notes once we're on the way."

Startled, I couldn't think of anything else to say; he had taken care of it all. I scribbled Mr. Guerin's address on one of my deposit slips and threw Mac my keys. He ducked his head and was gone. My old self resurrected itself one final time, and I ran to the steps, calling after him, "You better bring my old jeans and the blue leotard, too, in case this doesn't work out."